Midnight Promise

Dara Girard

ILORI
Press Books, LLC

Midnight Promise

Copyright © 2017 by Sadé Odubiyi

ISBN 978-1-949764048

All rights reserved. No part of this publication may be reproduced, stored in a retrieval system, or transmitted in any form or by any means, electronic, mechanical, recording or otherwise, without the prior written permission of the Publisher, excepting brief quotes used in reviews.

Printed in the United States of America
Cover photo © 2017 Nadiia Balytska/123rf
Cover and Layout Copyright © 2017 Ilori Press Books, LLC

This is a work of fiction. Names, characters, places, and incidents either are the product of the author's imagination or are used fictitiously, and any resemblance to actual persons, living or dead, business establishments, events or locales is entirely coincidental.

ILORI PRESS BOOKS, LLC
PO Box #10332
Silver Spring, MD 20914
www.iloripressbooks.com

Other Books by Dara

The Black Stockings Society

Power Play

A Gentleman's Offer

Body Chemistry

Round the Clock

Return of the Black Stockings Society

Playing for Keeps

After Hours

A Private Affair

Just One Look

Henson Series

Table for Two

Gaining Interest

Careless Rapture

Dangerous Curves

Familiar Stranger

The Clifton Sisters

The Sapphire Pendant

The Amber Stone

Dear Reader

Dear Reader,

Welcome to the second book in the *It Happened One Wedding* series where the best part of the story is after "I do."

Have you ever known someone who just seems unlucky? They lock their keys in the car on the same day they're running late? They get their clothes caught in door or sharp corners?

Well, Dr. Naomi Mensah is one such woman. She has no time to think about romance when her world constantly seems to be falling apart.

Enter Sebastian Scott, a man she resists at first until she learns he's the one person she can't live without.

I hope you enjoy *Midnight Promise*.

All the best,

Dara

You can find out more about this series and learn about my other titles on my web site, www.daragirard.com

Chapter One

The strange noises in her bedroom should have been her first clue.

The noises should have alerted her to the fact that her life, as she knew it, was about to blow up in her face. But Dr. Naomi Mensah had been so tired after returning from her trip to Costa Rica for a conference, that the strange noises didn't register at first. The flight had been delayed and traffic hellish, but she was still happy to be back, a day before scheduled, to get work done. As much as she liked attending workshops and listening to experts in her field to find out about the latest discoveries and developments, she preferred to be working in her lab.

Her research lab was her haven and every day she looked forward to being there.

As she entered her one bedroom apartment, on the first floor of a remodeled three level apartment complex tucked away in a Maryland suburb, she'd only been thinking of slipping into bed as she dropped her suitcase in the cluttered foyer, stacked with old trade journals, newspapers and books she wanted to donate, but never got around to.

The noises rose and fell in a strange rhythmic pattern. Naomi immediately thought her housekeeper, Maya, was struggling to shift furniture so she could find areas to clean, although if Naomi had been more clearheaded, she would have known that scenario was unlikely. Maya James, a heavyset girl in her mid-twenties with a smile as bright as the moon on a clear night and a walk as slow as a snail stuck in honey, appeared to be allergic to any type of exertion. Especially dusting, washing and vacuuming. It was only after hiring her that Naomi discovered that Maya was the second cousin of the owner of the cleaning service.

But by that time, she'd been fooled by the younger woman's charming smile and didn't want to have to find someone else. Luckily, Naomi wasn't too particular in her housecleaning needs and felt Maya did a serviceable job and since Naomi was rarely home—she spent most of her waking hours at the lab—as long as the basics were taken care of, toilets cleaned, shower and tub scrubbed, kitchen organized, she didn't have any real complaints.

"Maya, I'm back," Naomi called out to her, hoping not to scare her as she headed to her bedroom. "I know it's early, but a main speaker wasn't able to attend, so I decided to come home. I just want to sleep so you can finish cleaning tomorrow." She opened her bedroom door and stopped when she saw two people in a position that made her face burn with embarrassment. "Oh, excuse me," she quickly said, before she closed the door and turned back to the hall.

Then she paused and realized she hadn't just entered the wrong room in a hotel, she was in her apartment. There were two people in her bed!

She swung open the door again. She clearly hadn't been loud enough with her first entrance because the couple hadn't stopped their activity. It looked as if they'd increased their amorous interaction.

Naomi's gaze dropped to the pair of dark trousers lying on the wood floor that sat next to a pair of orange and black striped boxers. *Did the man think he was a tiger?* Her gaze shifted to the bright pink bra on the bed post, black fishnets pooled beneath it. Maya's sturdy brown legs were wrapped around the man while he grunted like a boar, beads of sweat glistening on his bald brown head. The room smelled of warm bodies and expensive cologne.

"What is going on!" Naomi said, banging the door with her fist to get their attention. Her actions had the desired effect: The bed stopped squeaking, the moaning and grunting halted and two expressions of surprised disbelief met hers.

The man scrambled out of the bed with an agility that belied his large size. He wasn't exactly fat, but was soft enough around the middle to hint at a decades' long career sitting at a desk. As he pulled on his boxers, Naomi noticed a gold ring on one of his chubby fingers. She hadn't realized Maya was married to a man nearly twenty years her senior. She understood new adventures helped to keep a marriage fresh and alive, but didn't appreciate them finding it like this.

"Sorry," he said breathless. "Didn't realize it was so late." He quickly buttoned up his conservative, light green shirt.

"Just go," Naomi said.

He shoved on his shoes and grabbed his coat. Naomi impatiently waited for him to finish, half expecting him to kiss Maya on the cheek and tell her he'd see her later, but he didn't. Instead he reached inside his coat. It was only when he pulled out his wallet that Naomi finally understood the full picture.

The stranger wasn't Maya's husband, but a paying customer. Naomi snatched the crisp bills out of his hand before Maya could. "Thank you," she said, tucking the money in her jeans pocket. "Now go and forget you ever came here."

He nodded and left.

When Maya didn't immediately follow, Naomi turned to her. She knew the girl could move slowly, but her movements had become glacial. The man had already changed and left, but Maya was just latching up her bra. She still had a cream white blouse and black skirt to put on. "Why are you still here?" Naomi demanded

Maya reached for the blouse. "You haven't paid me yet."

Naomi folded her arms. "That's a joke, right?"

"I cleaned the kitchen. I mopped the floor."

For some wild reason, Naomi imagined Maya with the man making their way across the kitchen floor with every forward thrust moving Maya's bottom across the ground.

Naomi grabbed Maya's fishnets, heels and skirt then headed for the door.

"Hey, those are mine!"

Naomi opened her front door and tossed them out into the hallway. "I know."

"I can't go out there half dressed."

"Don't worry, nobody's looking. And if they are, you've got great legs." Naomi shoved a screaming Maya out the door and closed it while Maya continued her nasty name calling. She leaned against the wall and squeezed her eyes shut. Was this really happening? Did she really just see that?

A few seconds later, Naomi straightened when someone knocked on her front door. She sighed and answered, "What?"

Maya stood there and flashed her bright, beautiful smile. "Could you keep this between us?"

Naomi slammed the door closed.

Chapter Two

"And then what did you do?" Naomi's younger sister, Elia, asked at the reception of their cousin's wedding. The two women stood under the large, white canopy being pounded by an unexpected spring rain. The bride, looking as if she belonged on top of a five tiered wedding cake, dressed in an ivory gown with long lace sleeves, sat in the corner, tears streaming down her face. The wedding ceremony had been ruined by the sudden downpour and she refused to dance or be comforted because she felt her marriage was doomed. Three bridesmaids, dressed in matching neon pink and turquoise dresses, surrounded her, trying their best to ease her distress. The groom, dressed in a navy suit and patterned tie, stood to the side with his best man, smoking something that didn't look or smell like a cigarette, but everybody pretended was.

Naomi and Elia took little notice of the groom or the bride since they were used to their cousin's dramatics and knew with enough coaxing she'd soon be taking over the dance floor. So they busied themselves at the make-your-own flower station where guests were given printed instructions and could work with an array of spray mums, different colored roses and colorful ribbons and pins to create their own corsage or boutonniere.

Behind them, other guests ate and chatted at the various purple covered round tables with white decorative accents, or took to the dance floor.

Naomi grabbed another spray of mums, wishing she could forget the incident that had happened three days ago. "There wasn't much to do."

Naomi glanced at the teary bride then the groom. He had a similar build as the man she'd found in her bedroom and soon the image of the man's tiger colored boxers and big brown bottom, bobbing up and down in the air, crashed into her thoughts. She wasn't sure she'd ever be able to close her eyes again. She groaned. "I come back from Costa Rica to discover my housekeeper has been using my apartment as a…" She shivered unable to finish the sentence. "I have to move. God knows how long she's been doing this. How many men have been going in and out of my place?" Naomi grabbed a pin and pricked her finger. She silently swore and sucked on it. "This is a nightmare."

"I'm so sorry," Elia said, expertly tying a ribbon around her corsage. She was good at crafts. Naomi's younger sister excelled at most things domestic or otherwise. She was the kind of woman who could win a beauty pageant, garden prize and baking prize all in the same day. She was a slender woman of refined manners and taste, her black hair was pulled back in a chignon, the blue dress she wore complimenting her dusty cocoa skin.

Naomi, in contrast, could already feel the knot of her braid coming lose; her green dress was too tight and too short. It was a cocktail dress with a flared skirt she'd grabbed at some dress shop, which was more suited for a cocktail party than a wedding. She'd fallen for the shop owners' assurance that it was perfect for her and that the color complemented Naomi's walnut colored skin.

Naomi had none of her sister's refined traits—being all thumbs in a garden, a disaster in the kitchen and although some remarked on the prettiness of her brown eyes, few looked past the serious dark eyes surrounded by heavy frames and her boyish figure to notice.

Naomi checked her finger for blood then grabbed the pin again. "I've already had two men show up at my place."

"You can't stay there."

"I know," she said, pricking herself again. "And I also have to get a new bed."

Elia snatched the pin from her. "What is wrong with you? You're worse than Susan," she said, referring to her four-year-old daughter. "Use the ribbons instead."

"I was following the instructions." She pointed to the elegantly typed card. "It says—"

"I know what it says, but you can't do it. Remember when Mom tried to teach you how to use the sewing machine?"

Naomi cleared her throat, heat stealing into her cheeks as she recalled the incident. "I was young and I only needed a few stitches."

"You were seventeen and Mom wouldn't let me near a sewing machine for *years* because of you."

Naomi grabbed one of the red ribbons.

"Why do you need a new bed?" her sister asked.

Naomi wrapped the ribbon around the stem of her flowers, but one slipped out of her grasp and fell to the ground. "I found a strange man in it," she said, picking the flower up. "Do I need to tell you the story again?"

"No," Elia said, watching her sister struggle to bind the stems together before taking it from her and doing it herself. "I mean you could just change the sheets and…"

Naomi watched her sister's expert hand, refusing to meet her eye. "I got upset so after they left I…" She licked her lip and toyed with her necklace. "I cut it up."

Elia's hands paused; Naomi slowly lifted her gaze to meet her sister's stunned expression. "You cut it up?"

That had been Pete O'Connell's fault. After stripping the sheets, with the ferocity of a zealot eager to toss a witch into a bonfire, she'd gotten a call from her research assistant, Monica, apologizing and telling her that she couldn't be part of Naomi's project because she was going to be working with Pete instead.

The arrogant, two faced bastard had stolen yet another top research assistant from her. Naturally, she didn't let her disappoint show. She wished Monica the best then hung up, grabbed a pair of scissors and attacked the bed as if she'd found Pete with Maya's legs wrapped around him, his annoyingly smug grin wiped clean off his face. He also had a similar build as the man she'd found with Maya. Big and bald with a peppered beard and ruddy cheeks. "Are you happy now?" she asked with each stab. "You couldn't stop with just one?"

Elia snapped her fingers in front of Naomi's face, bringing her out of her memory. "You cut up your mattress?"

Naomi nodded. "Yes."

"Why?"

She didn't want to tell her about Pete, that would sound crazy. She shrugged. "I got angry."

"You know I could have used it."

"No, I didn't actually."

"Because you don't think about things like that," Elia snapped. "I told you that we had to reorganize our guest room for Barry's great aunt and that the headboard got broken."

Yes, she had, Naomi now remembered. She just hadn't paid attention. "I'll help you get another one."

"What a waste. Next time call me."

"There had better not be a next time."

"I didn't mean it like that." She sighed, wistful. "I always loved your bed. You have terrible taste in most things, but it was gorgeous. The oak inlay—"

Naomi frowned. "Terrible taste?"

Elia adjusted a flower in her corsage. "We both know that you spend more time in your lab than anywhere else. You'd be happy with just a cot if you could get away with it."

"Still that was a little harsh." Naomi glanced down at her dress. "I even tried to look nice tonight."

Her sister patted her affectionately on the arm. "I know you tried and it shows."

Naomi paused not sure if that was a compliment or insult. Her sister eventually made it clear when she added, "You're lucky the dress isn't pink or you'd end up looking like a flamingo."

Naomi pulled a face, but decided not to care. Was it her fault she'd gotten their father's skinny legs? "Besides, I only got rid of the mattress not the entire bed so you weren't going to get it anyway."

A woman in a large orange hat, tottering on black heels that were accented with a flower design at the ankle latch, with a gait that made her look as if she were constantly walking on egg shells, approached them. "What are you two doing over here? You should be comforting your cousin. She's in such a state."

Naomi looked at her cousin who was now wiping her tears with a handkerchief. "She just wants the attention, Mom. It's not as if it's her first wedding."

June Mensah kissed her teeth. "Who are you to talk? At least she's had two husbands," she said, holding up two fingers as if it were a crude gesture. "You can't even get one."

"I don't want one."

"Quiet!" June said, then looked to the right and the left as if to make sure no one overheard. "If you speak like that, people will believe you."

Naomi feathered the petals of a mum. "Which is exactly the point."

Her mother patted her cheek, a look of sympathy crossing her handsome features. "Don't worry, my darling, your time will come."

"Mom, you're not listening. I don't—"

"I see you're wearing your aunt's necklace. You finally got the clasp fixed like I told you?"

No. "Of course," she said. She'd intended to, but the task kept escaping her mind and after the housekeeper incident, she had completely forgotten about fixing the clasp before she'd chosen to wear it. It was an expensive gift from her aunt that her mother had warned her about handling with care, but she didn't think it made much sense to keep something locked away that was meant to be worn.

Elia handed Naomi the now finished corsage. "Why did you wait so long to tell me?"

Naomi sniffed the corsage. "Not now," she warned under her breath.

"Tell you what?" June asked, gathering some flowers to create her own corsage.

"Nothing," Naomi said.

"She's traumatized because she found a man in her bed," Elia said.

Her mother's eyes widened. "Was he dead?"

"You watch too many dramas," Naomi said.

"You leave my dramas alone. Am I right?"

"No," Naomi said, giving her sister a fierce look. She hadn't wanted to let her mother know about the situation. She would only worry.

"Did you bring him home and forget his name?"

"Mom—"

June waved her hand. "No, that doesn't sound like you. I can't remember the last time you had a man in your apartment, let alone your bed. Did—"

"It was her housekeeper," Elia said.

"That Jamaican?"

Naomi pointed her corsage at her mother. "Says the daughter of Jamaican immigrants."

Her mother bristled. "You know what I mean. She was completely uncouth."

Elia snorted. "More than you know. Naomi found her baking someone's plantain in her oven."

June blinked then frowned. "You don't want her baking plantain in your oven?"

"No," Elia said with a giggle. "Maya put a man's plantain in her *personal* oven."

Her mother's frown deepened. She turned to Naomi. "What nonsense is your sister speaking?"

Naomi shook her head and feigned ignorance. "I don't know."

Elia released a heavy sigh. "The Jamaican—"

"She has a name," Naomi said.

Elia lifted a brow. "Does it matter now?"

"Yes, because—"

Elia turned to her mother. "She serviced a man in Naomi's bed."

Her mother blinked. "Served him what?"

Elia threw up her hands in exasperation. "Mom, why can't you understand subtly?"

"What's the use of being subtle when you can speak plain?" June shot back annoyed. "That's what your sister is good at." She looked at Naomi, expectant. "You tell me what happened."

"Mom," Naomi said with a sigh and brief shake of her head. "It's nothing."

Her mother set her gathered flowers on the table and folded her arms. "Your sister is spouting nonsense about nothing?"

"Yes."

Elia rested a hand on her hip. "Naomi found her housekeeper having sex with a man in Naomi's bed. Is that clear enough for you?"

June's mouth fell open. "She brought her man to your place?"

"That's where it gets worse. He wasn't 'her man' he was a client. She's a working girl. A prostitute."

"I know what a working girl is," June said, lifting her chin, offended.

"I wasn't sure," Elia said with a teasing grin. "Since you didn't understand my plantain analogy."

"Because that made no sense. How can you use plantains and ovens as a euphemism for sex?" She tapped her chin, thoughtful. "Although, now I can see the connection. But you know what would have been better? If you said Naomi found The Jamaican spreading her guava jelly over the man's—"

Naomi held up her hand, wanting to plug her ears. "Mom that's enough." It was enough to have to try to rid her mind of brown bottoms and striped boxers; she didn't want to add plantain and guava jelly to the mix.

June nodded with a knowing look. "I didn't trust her. Never trust a woman who dusts with her fingers. I once caught her using her palm because she was too lazy to use a cloth and—"

"Well, she's gone now."

Her mother suddenly covered her mouth in horror. "Dear God, to think she likely used that same hand on a man's cucumber. Your house could be covered in seeds!"

It was now Naomi's turn to look around to make sure nobody heard her. "Mom, please keep your voice down."

Elia giggled. "No one will know what she's talking about."

June clasped her hands together, her voice anxious. "You can't go home. What if there are other men there waiting? Did she put your address online?" Her eyes widened with renewed horror. "If so, then your address has gone international and you could have men coming from all corners of the globe!"

"I doubt that will happen."

Elia couldn't stop a grin. "Two men have already shown up."

Naomi glared at her sister. "Will you shut up?"

June pressed her hands against her cheeks, distress covering her face. "This is awful."

"Don't worry, Mom. I've changed the lock and I will be moving soon."

"Just wait until I tell your father. He'll know what to do."

"No, wait…" Naomi said, but her mother hurried away before she could stop her. She turned and hit her sister in the arm. "You're still a little snitch. Why did you have to tell her?"

Elia shrugged unrepentant. "What are little sisters for? At least she's not bothering you about getting married now."

"True."

They both looked at their cousin who was still crying.

"How long is she going to milk the attention?" Elia asked.

"Give her another ten minutes and she'll be fine," Naomi said, looking outside. "Plus it seems that the rain is easing up."

"She better get on the dance floor soon, because I don't know how high her new husband is trying to get," Elia said, nodding at the groom and best man whose mood and appetite appeared to have improved.

Naomi frowned. "Maybe Mom's right and we should go talk to her."

"There's nothing to say." Elia sighed. "Poor thing."

"I don't think it's that bad. The rain didn't ruin everything."

Elia shook her head. "No, I'm talking about your mattress. It finally gets some action and gets stabbed and tossed out."

"I don't need a man."

"It's been eight years. Are you sure it's not because—"

"You ended up marrying the first guy I ever dated seriously? No, I'm fine. I've told you this more times than I can count. You and Barry are perfect together. It never would have worked between us." She knew that people still felt a little sorry for her. That her younger sister ended up with the first and only man Naomi had ever brought home. But she didn't need anyone's pity. She'd met Barry Seagrove at twenty-two after completing her doctorate and saw dating as a new experience to try. He'd been a fellow student a few years older whose interest in biodiversity interested her.

It lasted four months. She felt relieved when they admitted that things wouldn't work out. She wasn't too surprised when a few weeks later he and Elia started going out. They'd hit it off at their first meeting with a passion she and Barry had never shared.

Naomi wasn't sure there was 'The Right Man' out there for her and didn't want to look. Others didn't understand her real passion—microbiology. They didn't understand that she felt alive looking at the life that abounded, which was invisible to the naked eye. They couldn't comprehend that the sight of microbes made her skin tingle, the magnificence of binary fission versus the process of mitosis, made her heart race.

Presently she was researching the correlation between the hepatitis C virus and kidney cancer; her focus being whether a carrier of the hepatitis C virus is significantly more prone to being diagnosed with kidney cancer than those without it. She was also interested in the ranging mutations of elephantiasis. No man could compete with that.

"I'm not like Mom," Elia said. "I'm not saying you have to get married, but you haven't even tried to be with someone."

"I don't need to. I'm not like you. I don't need shopping with the girls, wine tastings, book clubs and family vacations."

"True, but you do need a life."

Naomi pressed two fingers to her neck as if searching for a pulse. "You mean I'm dead?"

"I mean you need a life outside of the lab." She lowered her voice. "You're not taking care of yourself. You have bags under your eyes."

"That's because I haven't been able to sleep since—"

"No, you've had them before. And you've lost weight. Have you been skipping meals again? And without a bed, where do you sleep?"

"I have my power shakes. And I sleep on the couch." She rubbed her corsage underneath her sister's chin. "You're starting to sound like Mom. Don't worry about me," she said, although her sister's concerns reminded Naomi of her mentor, Dr. Vera Conklin, who'd urged her to attend the wedding 'just to be social a bit'. Naomi was known as a 'no show' at most family events, either from lack of interest or forgetfulness. She'd missed an uncle's housewarming party (she'd gotten absorbed in her research and lost track of time), her sister's baby shower (she'd gotten the dates mixed up) and her parent's twentieth wedding anniversary (same reason). Although she wasn't close to her cousin, aside from her mentor's urging, her mother's insistence and her sister's constant reminder, Naomi knew she had to attend the wedding or her mother's middle sister would have given her hell.

"Don't you think it's odd that you're rarely home; that you rarely pay attention to the real world around you, that your housekeeper could use your place for months without you knowing?"

"No, I don't. I love my work. And Maya is just…I should have gotten rid of her sooner." Naomi closed her eyes and groaned. "She worked for me for more than a year. How often do you think she used my place and I didn't know it?" She waved her corsage. "Never mind. Don't answer that. I just need to move out and put this all behind me." She turned to look at her cousin who was now on the dance floor with her new husband. "See? Everything turns out okay in the end. I'll be fine." But even as she offered her sister a smile, her words felt like a lie.

Chapter Three

She shouldn't have come. Her sister wasn't the only one to mention the dark circles under her eyes or her lost weight. She couldn't help that she was built like her Ghanaian born father— Dr. Abraham Mensah—all lines and angles without curves. And if they weren't worried about her appearance they kept reminding her how rarely they'd seen her. Yes, she travelled a lot. Yes, she worked long hours. Yes, she was still single. Was that a crime? Was it wrong to be ambitious?

Not that it was getting her very far since Pete had taken another researcher from her. What was the use of graduating from the University of Pennsylvania at eighteen, getting her post graduate training at the Stanford University School of Medicine if she wasn't making any strides? Why weren't people clamoring to work on her projects? Why was she thought of as second best?

Even the lab she'd been using had been shut down due to a mold outbreak. She was working in an interim facility, which housed seven other organizations—one a crystal healing center and the other an accounting firm. She felt like a failure compared to her father, who like his father before him, had graduated with honors from Oxford University, had served on several boards, won prestigious awards and wrote on subjects such as tuberculosis, elephantiasis and the mechanisms of acquired immunity. Although he had retired he was still a much sought after speaker.

Naomi spent the remainder of the night assuring her father that she'd be fine and he didn't need to escort her home, telling her cousin she made a beautiful bride and twice avoiding a man who thought her doctorate meant she was a physician and who wanted her to look at the suspicious mole on his neck.

By close to midnight she was ready to leave and happily made her escape into the cool spring evening, walking briskly through the parking lot. The rain had stopped, leaving the ground wet, the reflection of the moon shining in the puddles. She was looking at one such reflection when her heel caught in a grate and she stumbled forward.

She caught herself before she fell, but felt her necklace slip from her neck. She scrambled to reach it, but it slid through her fingers and clattered down the grate.

No, no, no. Please no!

Just what she needed. A bad week turned worse. She dropped to her knees, the cold, wet asphalt pressing against her skin.

This couldn't be happening.

Naomi touched her neck again, her heart sinking. The necklace was gone. Truly gone.

She pulled out her cell phone and used the light to peer into the dark black pit, hoping to see a glint of the gold chain reflected, but she didn't see anything. She tried to lift the grate, but it was heavier than expected and bit into her skin, causing her to yank her hands away and flex her sore fingers.

Naomi squeezed her eyes shut as her mother's voice rose in her mind, "I thought you said you finally got the clasp fixed like I told you. Do you know how much that necklace cost? Why are you so irresponsible?"

It wasn't that she didn't treasure it, she'd been careless, but it wasn't the first time. She'd ruined a silk blouse, a gift from her grandmother; a silver tea set she'd received from an uncle. But her aunt's necklace had been special. It had been a gift she'd given to Naomi when she'd gotten her first job. "A gift for all your accomplishments and the many more to come," she'd told her that day. And now she'd lost it down a sewer.

"Want me to get it for you?"

Naomi looked up and saw a man in shadow, the lamp-light illuminated behind him. She squinted, trying to make out his features. "I'm sorry?"

"You just dropped something, right?" he asked, his voice as deep and dark as the shadows around him.

"Yes."

"What was it?"

Naomi touched her throat again half hoping it would magically reappear. No, it was still gone. "My necklace."

"Do you want me to get it for you?"

Naomi pointed to make sure he understood the situation. "It fell down the grate."

"I know." He shoved his hands in his pockets. "Do you want me to get it for you or not?"

She wouldn't be too proud. She wasn't going to pretend she didn't need help. "Yes," she said feeling relieved. "Please."

"But I'll need a favor in return."

"Anything." She paused. She couldn't be too grateful. She didn't know who this man was. "As long as it's not illegal, immoral and it's within my power."

A smile entered his voice. "What's your definition of immoral?"

"I won't sleep with you."

"You think sleeping with a man is immoral?"

"Only when it's in exchange for certain favors," she said, her former housekeeper fresh in her thoughts. But she wished she hadn't mentioned it. *Why were they having this conversation when she just needed his help?* She stood to her feet, but still couldn't make out his features with the light behind him, the darkness still masking his face. "Those are my conditions otherwise you can leave."

He shrugged. "Fair enough. I'll get your necklace, if you promise to hire me as your assistant."

That didn't make any sense. "What kind of assistant?"

"Someone who helps you with your day-to-day duties. A personal assistant."

He needed a job that bad? She didn't need a personal assistant, and even if he'd wanted to be a research assistant, she wouldn't want to hire someone she'd just met in a parking lot.

Naomi shifted her gaze to the grate. But she did need her necklace back. "Okay."

He held out his hand. "Promise?"

She recoiled for a moment. His hand was enormous. She looked at what she could make of his shabby tux. Maybe he needed money. At least he was asking for a job. She would give him a good reward instead. She held out her hand. "I promise."

"Good." He lifted the grate as if he were lifting the lid off of a paper box and descended inside.

Naomi adjusted her glasses and paced. She chewed her nails and paced some more. Could he find it? Was it gone forever? How would she explain the loss of the necklace if he didn't? Her mother would never let her hear the end of it. "Can you see anything?" she called down to him, seeing the light from his cell phone.

"There's a lot of water, the rain didn't help."

She groaned. He wasn't going to find it. It was hopeless.

"But I'll get it, Mensah. Don't worry."

Mensah? He knew her last name? She didn't remember telling him. It didn't matter. He just needed to find the necklace. Naomi paced some more and as time passed her hopes faded. Soon she heard his feet on the metal ladder. She crouched down in anticipation. "Did you find it?"

He held out a slimy, dirty hand. "Here you go."

Naomi winced and recoiled both from the sight and the smell then gingerly accepted the sewage covered necklace. "Thank you," she said politely as he emerged, his suit covered in muck. He looked terrible and smelled even worse, but he'd done what he'd said. "I really appreciate it Mr…"

"Sebastian Scott."

"Thank you Sebastian."

He cleaned his hands on his trouser legs then reached inside his jacket. "I'll give you my card. So I can—"

"Naomi?"

She looked past him and saw her mother waving. She couldn't let her mother see her with this man or the necklace. She offered him a bright smile, snatched the card he held out to her and said, "I'll be in touch," hoping he'd accept her generous reward and she'd never see him again.

Chapter Four

His luck was about to change. Sebastian pumped the air with his fist as he walked into his house and headed for the kitchen. He now had a job with the illustrious Naomi Mensah. It had been worth pulling some strings to make sure he got invited to the wedding of the friend of his second cousin once removed.

"My God, you look awful," his mother said, coming into the room, her cane clicking against the cream tile floor. She'd been staying with him after recovering from hip surgery. She'd improved, but made no move to leave and he didn't want to push her. She'd been lonely since the death of his father five years ago. Although it was past midnight she looked as if she were ready for guests, draped in a silver colored silk robe and her head wrapped in a matching scarf, her mascara and lipstick still in place. But nobody had ever seen Josephine Scott without them.

Sebastian opened the fridge and grabbed an apple. "I met Dr. Naomi Mensah tonight."

"I thought you were going to a wedding."

He washed the apple and then took a bite. "I actually spoke to her and I'm going to be her assistant."

Josephine waved her cane at him. "You smell even worse than you look. At least consider the housekeeper and how much she'll have to clean up after you. You need to get changed right now."

Sebastian rested against the counter and sighed, staring up at the recess lighting that cast a soft light over the marble countertop, amazed by his good fortune. "I can't believe it."

"I'd hoped you would have met someone nice and you come back looking like a toad out of a swamp."

He took another bite of his apple and chewed thoughtfully. "She's better looking in person than her pictures give her credit for. Not that it matters. Hey!" he cried when his mother snatched the apple from him.

"Sebastian!"

He blinked. "What?" He took the apple back from her and frowned. "I'm standing right here, there's no need to shout."

"Did you hear a word I said?"

Nope. He glanced at his watch. "What are you doing up?"

"I couldn't sleep." She stared at his clothes. "What happened to you?"

"I just told you I met Dr. Naomi Mensah."

"Who?"

"Only one of the most brilliant minds in microbiology."

She motioned to his ruined suit with her cane. "You met her looking like that?"

"No, this happened after."

"After what?"

"I got her necklace out of the sewer."

"What was her necklace doing in the sewer?"

"It fell off her neck and I offered to help her and got a job in the process."

"You don't need a job."

That was true, but that was only part of his plan. "It's just the beginning. This will change things for me."

"Have you been drinking?"

"No, this is important. This is amazing. *She* is amazing. Better in person than I thought."

"Is she pretty?"

"I'm not sure, I didn't pay attention."

"You just said she looked better in person than in pictures."

"I was talking about her appearance in general. I wasn't making a specific classification."

Josephine curled her lip in disdain. "I hate when you start to talk like that. Knowing whether a woman is pretty or not does not take a detailed analysis."

"But pretty is relative. Whether I find her pretty or not is irrelevant if you don't think so, therefore I can't give you a factual assessment on a personal preference."

Josephine briefly shut her eyes. "Give me patience." She opened her eyes and spoke slowly. "Do you find her pretty?"

"I think so, but—"

"There is no 'but'. Stay away from her, you always get in trouble with pretty women."

"No, I don't. Besides, I plan to work with her not date her. She's published a number of articles." He paused. "Although, with two of them, I do question the veracity on the calculations used. She may have based her premise on a shaky foundation. However, her article on the—"

Josephine covered her ears and closed her eyes. "Sebastian!"

He took another bite of his apple. "You're shouting again."

She glared at him. "Because you're purposely avoiding the subject."

He frowned. "I am not. I thought the subject was Naomi Mensah."

"It is."

"And I was just telling you about—"

Josephine shook her head and slumped into a seat. "I don't care because I'm not interested. I don't want to see you get hurt again."

"I won't."

Josephine held up her hand and began counting her fingers. "Molly Robb, Kristine Lyle, Barbara Dean—"

He winced. "It's not like that."

His mother didn't need to remind him that he had terrible luck with women. It had started in middle school. That's when he'd first gotten his heart broken by Molly Robb who'd humiliated him in the school courtyard.

He'd been born with extreme clubbed feet that had taken multiple surgeries to fix. He'd spent most of his first eleven years in and out of hospitals so he'd been home schooled, but was thrilled to attend regular school. In middle school, he was in a wheelchair and chubby from lack of exercise and a love of food. He'd eaten to deal with the pain and the isolation, but was happy to be out of the hospital and with other kids.

Molly had been his first crush and she'd acted as if she liked him too with her cupid bow lips and shy smiles, so when she asked to meet him after school, so he could help her with her homework, he'd eagerly agreed.

He should have known when he saw her with her two girlfriends it was a set up. But he realized his mistake too late. They charged him, tipped over his wheelchair and laughed at him as he struggled to get upright. They recorded the event, eventually posting it on an online message board. For the first time in his life he wanted to crawl into the ground and hide, but he didn't. Instead he made it back into his chair and wheeled away determined not to cry.

He didn't know how his parents found out, if his brother had seen the video and told them or someone else, but soon after the incident his father came into his room.

Sebastian remembered not being able to look his father in the eye. He sat at his desk; wearing headphones blasting rap music with foul lyrics that made him feel empowered, pretending to do an equation he'd already figured out.

His father came up beside him, turned off the music and rested a large hand on his shoulder. "I heard about what happened in the courtyard."

Sebastian scribbled some numbers down, wishing he'd go away.

"I'm proud of you. You became a man that day."

Sebastian took off his headphone and stared up at him startled. "What?" He didn't feel like a man. He'd cried like a baby once he was alone in his room and didn't want to have to go to school again. For the past two days he'd stayed home saying he had a cold. He even considered asking his parents to home school him again.

His father squeezed his shoulder. "You made me proud," he said, the island lilt of his words filled with emotion.

Sebastian gritted his teeth. "No, I didn't."

"You didn't get back in that wheelchair and roll away?" his father asked surprised.

"Yes, but—"

"There's no 'but'. That's all life is. It's about getting knocked down and getting back up even when they laugh at you. Even when they hold your hand under their feet." He nodded at Sebastian's surprised expression. "Yes, I saw that too." He motioned to Sebastian's swollen hand where one of Molly's friend, the one with braces and straight black hair, had stood on it. "But you still got up. And you're going to keep getting up by being a success, by using that day as a ladder. As a weapon if you have to."

"A weapon?"

"Yes, a tool that will fuel you past all of them. Keep up your studies and you keep making me proud and you'll own the world. You're going to be taking over my business one day so get used to this."

Sebastian turned away and looked back at his math homework. He didn't look forward to taking over his father's real estate business.

"Do well this semester," his father continued, "and we'll visit your uncle this summer. Think you can do that?"

Sebastian twirled his pencil. He liked his Uncle and would love to visit his home in Trinidad, but he wasn't sure he could face his classmates again.

"You can't have a cold forever. Go to school and shame them with your knowledge."

Sebastian set his pencil down hard, wanting to snap it in two. He hated that advice. He hated his father always talking about the importance of being smart. He loved his father, but could also see how clueless he was. How clueless most adults were. Smart kids weren't liked and didn't make friends. But a summer away would be nice.

He rolled his pencil under his finger, pensive. A summer away with food and sun and beach seemed like a good trade. "Okay," he said and his father's promise galvanized him and helped him ignore the taunts and teasing he endured while he aced every subject.

That summer, the family visited his Uncle and Sebastian and his brother, Gregg, got to spend two months in a palm shaded house only yards away from the ocean. His uncle taught him how to fish and swim, which changed his life.

In the water he was free and powerful. Nothing could stop him and he also became engrossed by what he found in the water. The wildlife drew him in and that's when he knew what his life work would be.

But he still got in trouble with women. Kristine Lyle had been his college mistake. He was the only one who didn't know she was seeing two other guys at the same time and only needed him to help her pass her exams. Barbara had been more serious, he'd nearly married her. Until he found out she also wasn't what she seemed.

He had learned his lesson. His mother didn't need to worry about him. He knew that nothing would happen between him and Naomi. He needed the job to put his plan into action; she was a bridge to something bigger.

After five years, he had a chance at redemption. To reclaim the life he'd once loved. A chance to stand before his father's grave with pride.

Chapter Five

Someone was at the door.

Naomi glanced at the clock and scowled, she wasn't expecting anyone. She never accepted visitors before noon and she was only home because of a slight cold that she didn't want to pass to others in the lab. She'd been lazing on the couch wearing a pair of worn jeans and a white long sleeved shirt, reading one of her industry journals when she heard the doorbell.

The time on the clock said noon on the dot.

The two other men seeking an afternoon quickie had come around noon time. She really needed to move.

The bell rang again.

"Are you going to get that?" her father called from her bedroom that she now only used as a place to park her computer and extra research material. He'd come by to make sure that Naomi was safe. Her mother had already hired a crew to clean her place from top to bottom—whispering to her that cucumber seeds could be everywhere!—and didn't want Naomi left home alone with a cold since she was determined not to stay at her parents' place.

Her father had graciously agreed to look over some data with her and discuss another project she was interested in.

"Yes," she said, then shuffled over to the door. Her scowl increased when she looked through the peephole. Just as she expected. A man. Probably on his lunch break wanting Naomi to put a smile on his face.

She swung the door open and glared up at the large shaggy looking man in his mid-thirties who wore a suit that looked like it had never seen an iron. He had skin the color of roasted peanuts with maroon, square glasses, and nice brown eyes. He needed a haircut and a shave or at least a trim and some semblance of being groomed.

If she were to label him a bacteria it would be the the *lactococcus lactis,* a spherical-shaped bacterium mostly known for use in the production of buttermilk and cheese, but which had most impressed her because it was the first genetically modified organism to be used alive for the treatment of human diseases.

He looked like the kind of man who could both spoil something or improve it, depending on his use. But that didn't matter. He didn't have a delivery package, or a clipboard for her to sign, just a cumbersome looking black bag, possibly filled with sex toys. She couldn't imagine what kind of fantasy he was in the mood for, but she could guess that he'd come to her front door to spoil her day.

He cleared his throat. "Hello, I—"

His voice didn't suit him. His tone was distant but polite, a well modulated baritone as if he were ready to give a presentation, not spend a half hour with a prostitute. Naomi rested her hip on the door and shook her head, interrupting him. "I'm not here to judge you, but you've come to the wrong place. Maya is no longer offering her lunch or afternoon special. So if you could tell the others the same, I'd really appreciate it. Have a nice day." She closed the door and wiped her hands, pleased with herself. When the first two men had arrived, she hadn't been half as nonchalant. She'd shouted at the first one and the second guy— who'd given her a once over and said "You're a bit skinny for my taste with no boobs, but I'll stay if you give a discount"—she'd cursed out, using language she'd invented. So this new guy was lucky.

The doorbell rang again.

Or stupid.

It rang a third time. A fourth time.

Boy, the bastard was insistent. She opened the door.

He adjusted his glasses and cleared his throat. "There must be a mistake."

"There's no mistake. You're not the first to be confused, but you're wasting your time and mine. Now get out of my sight before I call the police." She slammed the door.

Her father poked his head out of the bedroom. "Are you okay?"

"Yes, I'm fine."

"Who was that?"

"No one." She was not going to explain the situation and have him calling her mother. Her mother would try to convince her to move within the next two hours. She didn't want to stay at their house. She loved them to bits, but her mother could nag. Every hour of the day she would be in her space. "Is that all you're going to eat for breakfast?" "Have you washed your hair?" "Are you really going to wear that again?" Naomi shivered at the thought. No, she'd deal with the men until she could find somewhere else to live.

The man rang again and knocked on the door.

"Please, there's been a mistake," he said in a rush when she opened the door. He pulled out his wallet. "I just—"

Naomi's temper snapped, remembering the other man waving cash in her face. "Do you want to go to jail? Do you want me to tell you what I think about men who go out with women behind their wives'…" She glanced at his hand and didn't see a ring… "or girlfriends' backs?"

He sighed and looked pained. "Dr. Mensah."

She froze. He knew her name? And why did his voice suddenly sound familiar?

"I'm here about the job," he continued.

Naomi held up her hand. "That's what I'm trying to tell you. Please listen closely." She leaned towards him and slowed her words, making sure to emphasize every syllable. "I don't do blow jobs or hand jobs or lube jobs. I'm trying to tell you that you've come to the wrong place."

She grabbed the door, but this time he stopped her before she could close it. A shiver of fear coursed through her as she met his hard, dark gaze. His glasses didn't soften his features. He looked large and strong and dangerous. Like a virus invading a cell with the ability to replicate until the cell was destroyed. He could overpower her swiftly and without effort.

She could scream, but she didn't want to put her father's life in danger. This man could easily overtake him. She licked her lips, her mouth dry. She'd make him calm down and then she'd find a weapon. She couldn't show fear.

But something must have registered on her face, because his grip loosened on the door and his expression softened. "I'm not going to hurt you." He held up his wallet to show her his driver's license. "I wanted to show my identification. I'm Sebastian Scott. I'm here to work for you."

She paused. "Me?" Had her mother hired a bodyguard and not told her? He didn't look the part, but his presence would certainly help.

He looked a little rueful. "I guess you forgot."

"Forgot about what?"

"To call me. It's been nearly a week. I'm your new personal assistant."

Naomi furrowed her brows. "I don't need an assistant."

"But you have one now, you promised me the night I retrieved your necklace."

Oh God…the necklace! The man! The sewer! It all came flooding back. Naomi had pushed the memory away as part of an awful dream. He'd even given her his card; it was probably buried deep in her glove compartment where she'd tossed it.

But he was here now and he really wanted to work for her. But he was all wrong. Pete gets a top assistant like Monica and she gets some guy who likes climbing into sewers. Her luck was truly terrible.

"Don't worry," Sebastian said, making his way inside, walking with a distinct stride she'd never seen before. "I'll make your life easy and won't be a bother. You won't regret this." He closed the door behind him, making it clear he didn't plan to leave. "I went to your lab first, and heard you were sick with a cold, so I brought some soup." He patted the black bag beside him. The one she'd imagined carried whips and chains.

"I have a very busy day today," she lied. "Could I call you back, um…?"

"Sebastian," he said patiently. "Sebastian Scott. And I'm ready to get started right now. Where's your kitchen? I'll heat the soup. Have you eaten?"

"No, but—"

Her father came into the room. "Naomi?" he said, his look and tone unsure, giving her a silent question of whether he should call the police.

"Dad…um this is…"

"Sebastian," the newcomer said, holding out his hand, his face spreading into a warm smile. "And it's an honor to meet you, sir. I attended your lecture in London."

"Thank you. I haven't been doing as much travelling in a while so that must have been quite some time ago."

"Doesn't matter. It was still memorable. Your take on—"

Naomi wrapped an arm around her father's, amazed by the scene of the two men—they looked like a large bear shaking hands with an antelope. "Sebastian, will you excuse us a moment?" she asked, but didn't give him a chance to reply as she led her father into the kitchen.

"He seems like a nice fellow," he said in approval. "That's a relief. I was afraid he was one of—"

Naomi took off her glasses and covered her eyes. "I did too." She let her hand fall and shoved her glasses back in place. "I made a mistake."

"That's okay, I'm sure he'll understand once you explain it."

She shook her head. "No, not about that."

"About what then?"

Naomi paced a moment then paused and rested her hands on her hips. "I promised him a job. I know it sounds crazy, but…I got into a bit of a jam and he helped me and…he's milking a moment of weakness. I'm sure he just wants money. I was going to send him a reward, but I forgot. So now he's here and I'll—"

"He was at my lecture."

Naomi paused and stared at him. "Dad, that has nothing to do with what I just said."

"Yes, it does. You're implying that he's here for dubious reasons. I don't think he is. If you hadn't interrupted him, he would have expanded on what he got from my lecture."

"I'm sure he's just flattering you. It's easy to read up on people nowadays. He knew my name that night. It could be a con."

"What night?"

"At the wedding. He was there. We met in the parking lot."

Her father folded his arms. "And you promised him a job. So you must honor it." He wagged a finger at her. "I brought up children who keep their word."

"Have you looked at him? How can I have a man like that follow me around as my assistant?"

"So you're going back on your promise?"

"It's not that simple."

"Yes, it is." He peeked out the kitchen and glanced at Sebastian sitting in the living room. "I wonder what's in the bag."

"He brought me soup."

"Hmm…I love soup. What kind?"

"I don't know. Probably chicken noodle. He knows I have a cold. But that's—"

"Even better. Tell me when it's ready." He headed for the door. "And you'd better keep your word to that young man or I'm telling your mother you're moving in with us." He flashed a smile then left.

Chapter Six

Naomi groaned and walked into the living room like a condemned woman. She sat in front of Sebastian. "We haven't talked salary. I don't—"

He stood. "Is the kitchen free now? You're looking a little peakish."

"Yes, but—" She stopped when he walked past her.

"Did you have breakfast?" he asked, setting the bag on the kitchen table. "Probably not," he said, answering his own question. He unzipped the bag and began to unpack a large container of soup, fresh bread, fruit salad, and a thermos. "Where are your bowls?"

She pointed to one of the cabinets. "But you really don't have to…" She stopped when he opened the lid of the soup, which was still piping hot, steam rising up to the ceiling. The soup wasn't the usual broth with bits of chicken and carrots and noodles. This was Caribbean style heaped with chicken, dumplings, yams, and potatoes and the spicy scent called her forward. It would be a shame to let such a meal go to waste.

Sebastian set the bowl in front of her then lifted an eyebrow. "Bread?"

"Yes, please." She didn't realize how hungry she was until she took the first taste. She'd missed breakfast. He was annoyingly right about that. She usually forgot about meals until someone reminded her, but her empty stomach rejoiced. "This is delicious."

"If you want more, just let me know."

She took another large spoonful. "No, this is fine." She paused then glanced with guilt at the remainder in the container. If Sebastian also ate, there wouldn't be enough for her father. "You gave me a lot. Let me put some of this away."

"I already ate. There's plenty for your father."

"Good," she said in relief.

He leaned back in his chair and studied her. "So what just happened?"

"What?" she said with little interest, solely focused on eating as much of the savory soup as possible. If she could inhale it she would.

"Why did you think I came for a blow job?"

Naomi choked on her soup and coughed.

Sebastian opened the thermos and poured a drink that smelled like lemon and lime. He held it out to her. "Here."

She waved him away. "No, I'm fine," she said then coughed again and changed her mind, taking the drink and gulping it down. She cleared her throat, her cheeks burning from embarrassment. He had a right to bring up her misunderstanding, but she still wished he hadn't. Couldn't he have pretended that she hadn't made an idiot of herself?

"I'm really sorry about that. I've had a few unwanted visitors."

"To put it mildly." He folded his arms and leaned back further, tilting the chair to balance on its back legs. She heard the chair groan under his weight. She hoped it would continue to hold him. She'd gotten the kitchen set secondhand and had no idea how old it was. He dwarfed the metal chair, with its curved back and tan cushion, so much so it seemed to disappear beneath him, giving him the eerie appearance of floating in mid-air.

She sighed and returned to her soup, she'd finish it before she sent him on his way. "The truth is I'm really overwhelmed right now. I have to find a new place to live and break my lease and—"

"I'll take care of that for you. Do I need to take care of a spiteful ex as well?"

Her head shot up, the spoon halfway to her mouth. "What?"

"Is there a reason men have been showing up at your door asking for sex?"

She swallowed. He was very straightforward. She liked that in a person, even if it was humiliating.

"My housekeeper." She shook her head. "I mean my *former* housekeeper, invited men here while I was away on business and probably even when I stayed overnight at the lab. And let's just say I work late a lot." Naomi set her spoon down and pushed the bowl away, losing her appetite at the thought of how long or how many men had seen the inside of her apartment. She held her head in her hands. "It's awful."

Sebastian pushed the soup towards her. "It's a problem that can be solved. Eat up."

She picked up the spoon then set it back down. "Not that easily."

He lifted the spoon.

She started to laugh. "Are you planning to feed me?"

"If I have to. You look exhausted."

And she felt it too. She felt as if the weight of her worries were about to crush her.

Sebastian put the spoon in her hand. "Come on. I'm here to help. Let me do my job."

"We haven't even discussed—"

"You can argue while you eat."

Naomi frowned then took a spoonful. Within seconds the warm concoction made her feel like her worries were melting away. Or was it him? His steady, quiet yet forceful presence was oddly comforting. She took another sip.

Sebastian nodded pleased then pulled out his cell phone. "What do you need?"

"What?" She put down her spoon, but when she saw a slight frown touch his lips, she picked it up again. "No, you can't..." She took a spoonful and saw the frown ease. "I mean I can't..." She took another bite and the frown disappeared and he unfolded his arms. "I know what I promised, but I don't have the funds to pay you. Even if it's a stipend, it would be stretch."

He leaned forward, setting the chair down on all four legs with a thud. "That's fine, then I'll be your personal assistant on a volunteer basis."

"But—"

"You haven't touched your bread." He shifted his gaze to his cell phone. "Now just tell me what you need." He stood. "Never mind. I'll be right back."

Moments later her father entered the kitchen with a big grin of his face. "Sebastian told me you'd be here." He grabbed a bowl and spoon. "Does it taste as good as it smells?"

"Where is he?"

Her father ladled soup into his bowl, sat down and began to eat. "Hmm…"

"Dad?"

"What?"

"Where is he?"

"He's just looking around."

"Why?"

"How am I supposed to know that?"

Before Naomi could leave the kitchen to find out what Sebastian was up to, he appeared in the doorway. "You don't appear to need much space or light for that matter."

Her father laughed. "That's true. I sometimes call her my little mushroom."

Naomi winced, that wasn't exactly something she wanted shared, but it was the family joke that she flourished best in dark, damp places. She couldn't remember the last time she looked outside her apartment window and wasn't even sure how many she had.

"Are you doing any university work? Do you want a place within walking distance?"

"No, at least for the next several years. I've won a grant," she said mentioning the project that had been funded by a foreign foundation due to the narrow scope of her research and lack of interest from the greater science community. "But…I'll be looking for another lab location since the present one won't work for what I plan to do."

He nodded. "Done."

She blinked. "What?"

"He said 'done'," her father said.

She shot him a glance. "I know what he said, I want to understand what it means."

"I know the perfect place," Sebastian said. "I can show you when your schedule is free." He held out his hand. "Let me see your phone."

"Why?"

"So I can see your schedule."

Naomi quickly finished her soup and set the bowl and spoon in the sink then left the kitchen. "I don't keep it there," she said as he followed her to the living room. She sat on the couch.

Sebastian sat in front of her. "Fine, then show me your calendar."

She shook her head.

"Your organizer?"

She shook her head again.

He frowned. "Then where do you keep your schedule?"

She tapped the side of her head.

"And how many flights have you missed?"

She paused again surprised by his perception. "Just two. Okay five, but…"

"And conferences?"

"I get to them just fine. Okay," she admitted when he looked doubtful. "So I usually miss the keynote speaker."

"Meetings? Movies? Dinner dates?"

"I don't date."

"Duly noted."

She cleared her throat wondering why she'd felt the need to mention that. It was none of his business, but it still irked her that he didn't seem surprised. She doubted his social life was better than hers.

"What does your girlfriend think about this?" She could have said boyfriend or tried for a neutral term, but decided to go with the law of percentages on the total number of asexuals and homosexuals versus heterosexuals and hazard a guess.

"She's fine."

Bingo. She felt pleased she'd pegged him correctly. Perhaps a little too pleased. She stiffened. It shouldn't matter one way or another. So what if he was smart, detailed, and thoughtful? With a haircut and a pressed suit he wouldn't look half bad. She mentally shook her head. What was she thinking? She'd never thought of a man like this and he was here for a job and probably had a girlfriend who alphabetized her pantry and color coordinated her shoes and purse. "I bet she's organized."

"She would be if she existed." Before she could say anything more, he changed the subject. "So you don't write anything down pertaining to your day-to-day activities?"

Naomi glanced around the sparse room where a bookshelf stacked with textbooks stood next to a dusty green standing lamp. "I have a calendar somewhere."

"That you clearly don't use. Don't worry. What's on the agenda today?"

"I was finishing a project with my father. I just came back from Costa Rica so…"

"Still unpacked from the look of the bags by the door."

She followed his glance. Nearly a week later and she'd practically forgotten about them. It wasn't unusual for a few weeks to pass before she put things away. "Do you want me to take anything to the cleaners?"

"Yes." She shook her head. "No." She held out her hands. "I really appreciate this. You're fast and efficient and

I could use some help now that Maya is gone. But I hardly know anything about you."

"That's why I gave you my card." He tapped his leg. "You can look me up right now if you want."

She'd do that later, having him sit there waiting would be too awkward. "Why do you want this job?" she said suddenly feeling like a rattled HR recruiter. "No, first how did you know my name?"

"I saw you at the wedding."

"Yes."

"And I couldn't help overhearing that you might be in need of help."

She cringed. "You heard that?"

"Your mother sounded like you were on the verge of being murdered."

"Yes, well…wait. Then why did you ask me why I said what I said to you at the door?"

He flashed a quick grin. "I wanted to hear you explain it yourself."

Naomi narrowed her eyes and crossed her legs. *Sneaky.* "So you're only here to help."

"Plus, I'm a big fan."

"Fan? I don't have fans. Maybe you have me confused with someone else. I'm…"

"Dr. Naomi Mensah," he said then proceeded to give her a brief description of her academic background and accomplishments as if he were writing her profile for Wikipedia.

She nodded semi-impressed. "You did do your homework."

"I've read your work."

"Then why would you want to be my personal assistant? Since you attended my father's lecture you must know something about the field. What's your specialty?"

He looked at her for a long moment, his sharp brown gaze both patient and probing. "My name is Sebastian Scott."

"Yes," she said with impatience. "I know. You told me."

"*Dr.* Sebastian Scott."

He waited, his probing gaze becoming more intense, as if he expected her to know the answer to a riddle. Was his name supposed to mean something to her? He was at the wedding. Were they family somehow? Distant cousins? No, her father would have known him too or her mother would have mentioned him. *Sebastian Scott.* For some reason his name did sound familiar. She bit her lip and swung her foot. "The only Sebastian Scott I can think of is the disgraced scientist whose lousy research caused BioCorps millions and led to his dismissal under a cloud of shame."

He blinked.

Naomi silently swore as her eyes widened. *Ohhhh…noooo…* "That's you?"

He blinked again.

"But—"

"We can talk about me later. You should probably rest now so you can recover from your cold. I'll be here tomorrow at eight sharp."

"But it's Saturday."

"That's fine." He walked to the door. "We need to find you a new place to stay. It will be a pleasure to work with you." He nodded then left.

Chapter Seven

Naomi stormed into the kitchen where her father was finishing his soup with relish. She gestured to the other room. "Did you hear that?" she said with a note of panic in her voice.

He licked his lips. "Is there enough of this soup to take home to your mother?"

"Dad, did you just hear that!"

"Hear what?"

Naomi fell into the chair in front of him. "Dad! That was Sebastian Scott. *The* Sebastian Scott. Dr. Disgrace. Sebastian the—"

"And what do they call you?"

"Besides brilliant?"

"The other name. Isn't it Nutty Naomi?"

She frowned. "I didn't know you knew it too."

"Nicknames have no business in our field, they belong on playgrounds and sometimes not even there. I expect better from you."

"Okay, so I won't call him a name, that doesn't change who he is."

"At least one problem is solved."

"What is that?"

"I wondered why he seemed familiar, and now I know why. He didn't lie about attending a lecture of mine and he would know who you are. So he's not a con or crazy, although he's let himself go a bit."

Naomi's brows shot up. "A bit? He needs to shape his hair and trim his beard and, his clothes don't fit him well and are crumpled. He looks like he's dragged himself out of a cardboard box."

Her father shook his head in regret. "Dr. Scott had such promise. He'd risen faster than most. It's a shame."

It was a shame. There had been such hope in the research he and his team had developed. Their data helped create a synthetic antibiotic against the tuberculosis bacterium. Unfortunately, it had a deleterious effect on the ear and caused impaired hearing. It had been rumored that in a push to produce the antibiotic, results had been doctored or interpreted with lack of care.

"I can't work with him."

"You made—"

"I know what I said, but my reputation is everything. I can't be seen with him. And why would he want this job anyway? He should be teaching high school somewhere. Or selling insurance."

"Insurance?"

She waved her hand in a dismissive gesture. "I couldn't think of something else."

"You can't back out now. He can find you a place."

"So you were listening."

"Only to that part. Your mother is very worried. The sooner you're out of this place, the sooner I can go back to my regular routine."

"You're retired."

"I still have a regular routine. I had to miss playing tennis because of this." He met every week with his close friend Dr. Khan. "And I want to make progress on my book."

"I wonder what he wants?"

"You'll have plenty of time to find out."

Naomi pressed her hands together as if in prayer. "Dad, please, you have to help me get out of this. I can't be seen with him."

"You can and you will. What 'jam' as you call it, did he help you out of?"

She let her hands fall and sank back in her seat. "It's nothing."

He stood and put his bowl in the sink. "Maybe I should ask him."

"No, don't," she said quickly. She sighed resigned. "Fine, I'll work with him." *Until I can find a way to get rid of him.*

Chapter Eight

He still couldn't determine whether she was pretty or not. Sebastian tapped a finger on his desk in his study while a grandfather clock ticked in the background. The afternoon sun slipped through the blinds behind him causing striped shadows to fall across the floor.

Sebastian rested his palm flat on the table, perplexed. His mother's question should have been a simple one, but he couldn't answer it yet. Was she pretty?

Dr. Naomi Mensah had arresting, angular features that on their own could be off-putting—a pointed determined chin, sharp cheekbones, short, straight eyelashes—but put together in her oval face he found himself intrigued by her snapping brown eyes and full lower lip. He found himself watching it as she ate, watching her pink tongue sweep across it after a spoonful of soup. That tongue could keep him up at nights.

A knock on the door woke him out of his wandering thoughts. He cleared his throat, trying to ease the heat and tension in his body. "Come in."

His friend and personal secretary, Andre Bremmer, came in bristling with indignation. Sebastian wasn't surprised, he'd expected the response. "I can't let you do this," Andre said.

Sebastian sighed. "You spoke to Mom."

"She's in a panic. She thinks you've lost your mind."

"I haven't. I've already completed my first assignment."

Andre sat down and waved his hands. "But this doesn't make any sense."

"It makes perfect sense to me. And you know me better than to think I'd do anything irrational."

"I still can't let you do this."

Sebastian smiled, amused. They both knew it was an empty threat. There was nothing Andre could do to stop him. Sebastian was a head taller and fifteen years younger than Andre. A hard looking, greying man with a bulldog face and the tenacity to match. His father had hired him first, eight years ago, but he and Sebastian became fast friends so when his father grew ill, Sebastian hired Andre as his personal secretary. He managed the house and completed other duties for Sebastian and Josephine.

"I'll give you back the money," Andre said.

Sebastian's smile fell. He'd given him an extra bonus to compensate for having to look after his mother while Sebastian put his plan into action. "No you won't. You have a family to support."

"And you've always taken good care of me and my family."

He nodded. "I always will."

"And it's my job to take care of you."

"You don't need to do that for a while. An assistant doesn't need another assistant. It will just look ridiculous. When's the last time you took a vacation? You look like you could use one. I'll get someone to look in on Mom."

"I don't need a vacation, I like what I do. You can't be an assistant to that woman."

Sebastian's patience began to fade. "That woman is a highly respected—"

"I know what she is. But this situation is beneath you."

"You're the only person who thinks so."

"A waste of your genius."

"Again arguable."

"What would your father say?"

Sebastian shrugged. "Considering he's dead. Not very much."

"Why would you do this? You've suffered enough. Why punish yourself even more?"

"This isn't punishment. This is an opportunity."

"How?"

"I have my reasons. But just know this, there are certain variables in place that increase the probability of success."

Andre blinked, confused.

Sebastian adjusted his glasses knowing he needed to speak more plainly. "I know what I am doing."

"We can't ignore the elephant in the room."

"Which is?"

"She looks a little like Barbara."

"She looks nothing like her. The only similarity is that they're both black and wear glasses."

"But you have a type."

Sebastian slid his finger across the table from the left to the right. "See this line? It's best not to cross it."

Andre ignored him. "The moment she entered your life is the moment things went downhill."

Sebastian clasped his hands together in resignation, trying to scare Andre rarely worked. He was one of the few people Sebastian couldn't intimidate. He clicked his tongue as if to scold him. "That's sloppy logic. You know better than that. Just because it rains the same day you wash your car doesn't mean washing your car caused the rain."

"She went off and married—"

Sebastian couldn't stop a grin. "That just shows she has terrible taste in men," he cut in not wanting to remember how Barbara had left him at a time when his father was dying and his career was at a crossroads, to marry a more established colleague who boosted her career.

Andre frowned. "You're not taking this seriously."

"No," Sebastian said with a laugh, "and I never plan to. It hurt. I got over it. Besides, Dr. Naomi Mensah is different."

"There are rumors."

"I don't listen to rumors."

"She's odd and in your field that's saying a lot. They say she's so focused that a marching band could pass her by with horns blaring and she wouldn't notice. That at almost every meal she uses a straw because her meals come in a thermos."

"I like a little eccentricity."

Andre's frown deepened. "She's not rich enough to be eccentric." He leaned forward. "I know it's been…difficult since your father's passing and having to take care of the business these past several years instead of working on what you want must have been a strain, but you're better off than most. If you hadn't had your father's business to fall back on, who knows where you might have ended up after what happened?"

Sebastian rested his chin in his hand looking bored. "If you have a point, I'd like you to get to it."

"Working with a scientist, isn't the same as being one."

He nodded. "Duly noted."

"And—"

Sebastian held up his hand. "This is where the discussion ends." He let his hand fall and smiled. "I have my reasons so relax. I haven't lost my mind. You worry too much."

"Because you don't worry enough."

"Tell Mom that the company is safe and soon Gregg will be able to take on more duties."

Andre nodded and left, but didn't feel reassured. If there was one thing he did well, it was worry. Growing up he worried where his next meal would come from; he worried about staying out of trouble; he worried about getting kicked around by his father who thought Andre's light brown skin meant his mother had stepped out on him; he worried about keeping his family together. But as he grew older he kept his worrying in check, to the relief of his wife and daughters, but when he did worry it was monumental.

And he was worried now. Sebastian used to trust him, used to confide in him, but he was keeping secrets and that couldn't be good. Andre didn't know what to do.

Josephine met him in the hallway, anxiety shining bright in her eyes. "Well?"

"He said he has his reasons," Andre said, wishing he had better news to tell her.

"Did he tell you what those reasons are?"

"No, but he seems determined. Give him space he may grow bored. Being an assistant isn't easy." He lightly touched her shoulder and offered a smile. "I should know."

Josephine didn't respond to his touch, her gaze growing more anxious. "Should we get his brother involved?"

"There's nothing he can do. The company is stable and Gregg is in a good position now. I don't think Sebastian would have planned something like this otherwise. Come, you shouldn't be standing like this." He led her to her bedroom.

Josephine sat on her chaise lounge chair and set her cane aside. "What do you know about the woman?"

"Everything I told you. Until we can understand his reason for choosing her there's nothing we can do."

"There's always something to do."

Andre shoved his hands in his pockets and rocked on his heels. "Right now, all we can do is wait and see."

Chapter Nine

D r. Sebastian Scott had clearly lost his mind. Naomi stood in the elegant room not knowing what else to think.

She'd expected a one bedroom apartment, not a suite inside a mansion. That Saturday morning, she'd prepared herself to have Sebastian help her look at a two story walkup or studio apartment on the eighth floor somewhere. When he drove her out of the suburbs to a curved driveway and an expansive home nestled on acres of land that looked as if it were designed for royalty, she had been confused.

Now she stood on the second floor staring at a master suite that could have swallowed her apartment two times over. It boasted high ceilings, large windows—*lots of light!* she could hear her mother squeal with delight—and was meticulously furnished.

"What do you think?" Sebastian asked. "Anything you don't like can be removed."

Naomi stared at the room in awe. "How many others rent here?" She'd counted the bedroom doors and could imagine seven to ten other tenants, but she didn't know what the lower level contained.

"You'd be the only one."

"Has the owner gotten into trouble and needs the ready cash of renters to cover the mortgage?"

"No."

She waited for him to expand further but after a few awkward seconds realized he didn't plan to say anything else. She walked into the full bathroom gaping at the elegant modern design and light effects to create a luxurious experience and then went into the bedroom where a double bed, chaise lounge chair and chandelier greeted her. She met him in the main area shaking her head, dumbfounded that he would even tempt her this way. "I can't afford this. All I need is a simple place to eat and sleep."

"The cost will be comparable to what you were paying for your apartment."

"That's impossible." She walked over to the bookshelf and gasped at the selection of titles—*The Andromeda Strain, Antimicrobial Agents and Chemotherapy*—it was as if the room had been created with her specifically in mind.

"You don't like it?" he asked in an odd tone.

She turned to him. "No."

He nodded. "Duly noted. I'll—"

She spread her arms to the side and threw back her head. "It's divine. I'm in heaven." She let her arms fall and looked at him. "And my sister thinks I have terrible taste, but if she saw me here she'd change her mind. But—" She wagged her finger at him when he opened his mouth. "It's too good to be true. I'm waiting for the other shoe to drop."

She noticed his jaw relax and realized that he'd been worried. How could that be? Who wouldn't love this place?

"Not many people would like that abstract," he said, nodding to a painting on the wall, by an artist who used cell patterns for his creations.

"I'd seen this work before. It's my favorite."

A quick smile came and then went. "Mine too."

She called him over with the crook of her finger.

He bent down. "Yes?"

She cupped his face in her hands. "Why didn't you warn me that you are crazy?"

"Crazy?"

"It's cruel to get a woman's hopes up like this. We aren't sure what the owner is like and whether he or she will even rent to me."

Sebastian clasped his hands behind his back and straightened. "This house is also close to the lab you'll be using."

Her brows shot up. "You found me a lab too?"

He nodded and turned. "Let's go see it."

She grabbed his arm, then quickly let go when he looked at her surprised.

And at that moment a sensuous light passed between them that startled her , causing her heart to beat fast and her gaze to hold his longer than she needed to.

"What do I have to do?" she asked, feeling suddenly breathless.

He frowned. "What?" he asked, his voice sounding deeper than before.

She swallowed and steadied herself. It was nothing. It was the beauty of the room. The light. She'd never been surrounded by so much natural light; it was making her feel heady. "What do I have to do for all this? Everything has a price." She bit her lip. "Things like this don't happen to me."

Sebastian folded his arms and gave her the long, measuring look that made her skin tingle. She couldn't read his thoughts although it was a look she was starting to get used to. He finally said, "The lab is mine and so is the house so you can stop worrying. You don't have to do anything but focus on your work." He turned.

She grabbed his arm again, but this time when he looked at her, she didn't let go, even though her hands trembled a bit from a mixture of anxiety, excitement and another feeling she couldn't quite place. "What you just said doesn't make any sense to me."

"Which part confused you?"

"All of it." She threw up her hands. "How can you own a lab? How can this be your house when you're—"

"A disgraced scientist who should be living in a boarding house eating canned beans? I'm sorry to disappoint you." He left the room.

She found him heading down the stairs. For a large man, he moved fast. She hurried to catch up. "It's just… Come on, few scientists—let alone ordinary people—live this well. What do you do?"

"I work for you."

"I wish you'd stop saying that."

"Why? It's true."

"That doesn't make any sense either."

"Sebastian is that you?" a female voice called from the hallway.

He halted so suddenly, Naomi bumped into him. She stumbled back catching herself with the railing; he didn't budge.

"Sebastian?"

He sighed then slowly headed down the remainder of the stairs.

"Who is that?" Naomi asked.

"My mother."

Naomi widened her eyes. "You live with your mother?"

"My mother lives with me," he smoothly corrected. "But we won't be in your way. She has a room on the main floor."

"Sebastian!"

His jaw twitched.

Naomi nudged him forward, surprised by his sudden leisurely pace. "She sounds like she really wants you. Maybe she hurt herself."

"No, she always calls me like that when I don't respond the first few times." He proceeded down to the main floor and walked into the sitting room where an attractive older woman sat.

"I thought I heard voices," she said in a pout. "Why didn't you say anything?"

"This is Dr. Naomi Mensah," Sebastian said. "She'll be staying with us for a few months."

His mother's mouth fell open making it clear she'd had no idea of this new arrangement. "And now I'm going to take her to the lab. Andre will be here to take you shopping in twenty minutes." He kissed her on the cheek. "Good-bye." His tone left no room for argument, although Naomi could tell from his mother's expression that she'd have plenty of questions for him when they were alone.

Naomi held out her hand. "It's a pleasure to meet you."

But his mother was too busy staring at her son in stunned silence to notice the gesture, so she took a step back and followed Sebastian outside.

"I knew it was too good to be true," Naomi said once they were in the car.

"My mother won't be a problem."

"She didn't look too pleased to see me."

He checked his rearview mirror looking unperturbed.

"And that doesn't bother you at all," she said in a dry tone.

"I think you're really going to like the lab."

Naomi actually squealed when she saw the lab. It was even more stunning than the house. It was state of the art, simple, clean. It even had a special keypad with the passcode 1872, the year Ferdinand J Cohn contributed to the founding of the science of bacteriology. "You're not my assistant," Naomi said. "You're my fairy godfather."

Sebastian smiled. "That's how I felt the first time I saw it finished."

"But you don't use it."

"I had plans…" he said, letting his sentence drift away, but not before Naomi heard a touch of longing in his voice and saw brief sadness in his eyes.

And at that moment she knew the house and money couldn't replace the loss of a career he'd loved. She wanted to know more. How could he have made such an error? Had he tried to correct it? What had really gone wrong?

Soon she found herself not only wondering about his career, but about the man himself. She suddenly felt drawn to him, noticing his broad shoulders and the elegant slope of his nose. It was the first time she'd seen him unhappy— she'd seen him confused, annoyed, frustrated, but not like this—and she didn't like the expression, so she brightened her tone and smiled and said, "We'll put it to good use. This day has been amazing. The house, the lab. Next you'll be replacing my car—"

His gaze sharpened. "Is your car giving you trouble?"

"No. It was just an example. But it's time we were honest with each other."

He nodded. "I haven't lied to you."

"No, but I don't need an assistant and you clearly don't need a job. Why even volunteer for a position like this?"

That distant, but polite look entered his eyes and she knew he was going to change the topic. He didn't disappoint. He turned and headed outside.

"As you can see," he said once they were through the main doors, "the lab is in an ideal location to walk to eateries and is accessible by bus or train if your researchers don't own cars. There's also a gym nearby, but at the house there's a pool I can show you later."

He had his reasons to avoid her questions and she wouldn't press him. Right now she was getting a better deal than he was. She'd find out his true agenda later. "A swimming pool wouldn't do me much good since I can't swim. I know, I know," she said when an expression of surprise crossed his face. "Graduate with honors from University of Pennsylvania at eighteen but I can't even do a duck paddle. I've put it on my life list to learn one day. What are you doing?" she asked when he started to type something on his cell phone.

"Making a note to find you an instructor. You'll never find time for things you don't schedule."

She rolled her eyes. "You and schedules."

But within two days she was already getting used to him. Actually liking him. She hadn't responded to a man like this in years. Maybe ever. Even in grad school, she'd only gone out with Barry out of curiosity. With Sebastian, she was more than curious—she was intrigued. He was like a new specimen she wanted to study. That wasn't good. She could become obsessive about things like that.

He'd helped her solve two major problems, but she didn't need a personal assistant so she'd have to get rid of him on her own.

Chapter Ten

Josephine hummed as the car sped down the street, finding the spring afternoon bright and beautiful in every way from the dot of clouds in the blue sky to the sight of purple poppies in a garden. She glanced at the back of Andre's head as he sat in the driver's seat, fighting a wild urge to kiss it in relief. She'd never been in such a good mood. So good, she was going to treat herself to a manicure.

"There's nothing to worry about," she told him. "Absolutely nothing at all."

Andre was quiet a few moments then said, "Why the change of heart?"

"I met her. That doctor woman he's been talking about and she's not a threat at all."

"I wouldn't be too sure of that."

"I am. I know my son."

"Then why do you think he chose her?"

Josephine sniffed. "When have I ever understood what my son was about? He's even letting her stay at the house."

"Yes, I know. I had to get the suite prepared." Andre met her eyes in the rearview mirror. "And that doesn't worry you?"

"I told you, I met her. There's no spark between them and she's nothing like Barbara. She's skinny as a twig and pretty enough, but not remarkable. And when I saw him with her, I could tell he wasn't attracted to her like the others. That's when I knew he was up to something. I should have paid more attention when he was talking about her work."

"He might be trying to find a way back into the field."

Josephine nodded. "Agreed. That's my suspicion too, but what could she possibly have that he'd want?"

"You want me to find out even more about her?"

"If it's not too much trouble," she said, which meant 'Find out as much as you can as soon as possible.'

Chapter Eleven

She couldn't get rid of him.

In the nearly two months they'd been together, Naomi had sent Sebastian on five useless trips to Eastern Shore and Anacostia to get micro-samples she didn't need. He didn't care. He returned and cataloged everything with the precision of a true scientist. Which bothered her. As detailed as he was, how could he have made such a huge error at BioCorps? But she fought to keep her curiosity at bay as she tried to figure out a way to get rid of him so she wouldn't grow attached.

Already she feared she was failing because he made her life easier. In the morning her breakfast was prepared, he took her to the lab where she convened with her research team, having gotten there without having to think about traffic, Sebastian then reminded her about lunch, which he also prepared (before him she'd often forget her lunch at home),then she'd work late into the evening. Her clothes were dry cleaned, he reminded her of a dentist appointment she'd forgotten about and even found a book she'd been searching for for months. He was becoming indispensable.

She couldn't have that. But she didn't mind it either.

Naomi stood in front of the abstract painting in her room, the early summer sun blocked by the velvet drapes she kept closed in order to concentrate. She couldn't understand her warring emotions.

She jumped when her phone rang. She checked the number; a little disappointed it wasn't him, then picked it up and sat on the couch. "Hello?"

"Your father wants to invite Dr. Scott over for dinner."

Naomi adjusted her glasses. "Why?"

"Because you haven't invited us over yet."

Naomi stretched her legs along the couch. "He's my assistant not my boyfriend, you don't need to formally meet him."

"I must thank him for the soup he had delivered to us, and that beautiful place where you're staying."

"He already knows you liked the soup. I had him give me the name of the restaurant, remember? And I'm paying rent, so it's not a complete charity."

"I didn't say it was."

Naomi swung her feet to the ground as a thought hit her. "Oh no, I haven't paid my rent yet." She closed her eyes and pounded her forehead with her fist. "How could I have forgotten that? I used to have it done automatically; I haven't set that up yet." She stood up and paced. "I'll have to tell Sebastian to...wait why didn't he remind me since he owns the place?"

"He's both your personal assistant and your landlord?"

Naomi silently swore. She'd been careful not to tell her mother the connection. When her parents had come to see where she was staying, she'd come up with an elaborate story of a wealthy, elderly woman who'd devoted her life to funding people in the scientific community and on an exclusive basis would let some take up residence in her home for a nominal fee over the course of a year. They'd believed her. "It's a long story."

"I like to hear it. Does he have any food allergies?"

Naomi sighed, her mother could be so stubborn. "I don't know."

"Is he a vegetarian?"

"I don't know."

"What does he like to eat?"

"I don't know."

"You've been with this man all this time and you don't know what he likes to eat?" her mother said sounding appalled.

Naomi felt properly scolded. To her shame she realized that she'd never seen Sebastian eat. He'd always made sure she had her three meals, but now as she looked back, he never ate with her. Why was that? How could she have only noticed that now? *You don't observe the world around you*, her sister had said.

"Call me back when you get the answers," her mother said.

"Don't be surprised if he decides not to come."

Her mother made a sound as if that were an impossibility then said, "We want you over this Saturday around six," before disconnecting.

At breakfast the next morning, Naomi tucked into spinached eggs and toast reviewing all that she planned to do for the day, wondering what the kidney cancer cells they had on slides would reveal today, when she paused to look across the table at Sebastian who was reading the complete collection of Beatrix Potter, which he did most mornings. She remembered teasing him about it once, and he just shrugged and said "I like the pictures" as if she were the one being childish and she never teased him again, especially after she snuck a peek and saw the artistic detail and skill in every painting and sketch.

But she was getting used to him surprising her and opening her eyes. She remembered the gorgeous bed and breakfast in Pennsylvania he'd found for her to stay in when she had a lecture at the university. The new gold lace red dress he bought her when she accidentally burned the one she was supposed to wear to a charity event with an iron (she'd gotten distracted by a statistics problem she was trying to figure out). When she asked him how much the dress cost, he refused to give her a figure, but she suspected it cost more than her entire wardrobe combined.

However, his generosity didn't end there. When her project funder came into town for a visit, Sebastian scheduled a dinner cruise on the Potomac, something Naomi would never have thought of. In truth, if she hadn't had Sebastian she would have forgotten he was in town entirely. She still remembered the sight of passing by the National Monument at night, while she enjoyed a Mediterranean couscous and chickpea salad and baked ziti pasta. She'd never forget how much she enjoyed finding out more about her funder—what his interests were, how much they had in common—and his wife, for the first time seeing a person behind the foundation.

When the funder went to the dance floor joined by his wife, she remembered that Sebastian stretched his hand out to her.

She looked at him alarmed. "What are you doing?"

"Asking you to dance."

"But I don't dance."

"You will tonight," he said, taking her hand and lifting her to her feet.

"I'm a terrible dancer," she said as he led her to the dance floor.

"That's okay," he said before he drew her into a dancer's embrace.

And in his arms he made it more than okay, within moments she felt as if she were floating on air, the feel of his hand in hers, the heat of the palm of his hand at the small of her back. When she was eight years old, she remembered being caught in a downpour with her father when they'd both gone for a walk. They returned home wet and shivering and as her mother dried her up with a towel, she scolded her father for not paying attention to the weather forecast and at least carrying an umbrella. Then her mother wrapped Naomi in a warm blue blanket and her shivering stopped and she felt secure and safe. She felt that same way now…with a little more heat.

Sebastian moved well and she moved well with him. And for a brief moment Naomi closed her eyes and imagined what it would be like to wake up beside him.

"Naomi," he'd say in a smooth velvet tone. And she'd just sigh and pretend to be asleep. He'd say her name again this time with a question and then he'd say her name a third time, nudging her awake.

She sighed when she felt the featherlike touch of his lips against hers. It felt so real…It took Naomi a second to realize it was. She opened her eyes and looked up at him startled. "Did you just kiss me?"

Her reaction seemed to amuse him. "Yes, I'm trying to wake you out of a dream. I said your name three times."

"Why?"

"Because the song is over."

She looked around and saw others dancing to the upbeat music. She pulled away from him, her facing burning. "I'm sorry."

"It's okay."

Naomi cast a nervous glance around the room to make sure her funder hadn't seen them. She didn't want to look unprofessional. Sebastian was her personal assistant not her boyfriend.

"Don't worry, they didn't see us."

"You didn't have to kiss me," Naomi said, heading back to their table, her lips tingling.

Sebastian pulled out her chair. "It wasn't a real kiss, just a quick peck."

She sat down. "It was a kiss."

He pushed her chair in. "Trust me," he said in a low voice, his breath hot against her ear. "If I were to really kiss you, you'd know the difference."

She swallowed, believing him. He was her personal assistant nothing else and right now he was just teasing her. She couldn't make it mean anything more than that. She pushed the dance and light kiss from her mind and enjoyed the remainder of the evening, indulging in a chocolate cake for dessert and chatting with her funder when he returned to the table. She hadn't paid much attention to Sebastian, determined to pretend he had no affect on her. She didn't even notice if he ate anything or not.

As she studied him now at the breakfast table, it took her a few seconds to notice she was the only one with any food. He didn't even have a cup of coffee or a glass of water.

It was true. She'd never seen him eat before. *Ever.* She didn't even know where his room was. What time did he go to bed? Did he shower in the morning or take a bath at night? She still knew so little about him.

"If you want to make yourself some toast, I don't mind being a little late," she said, her stomach tightening. She hated being late and itched to be in her lab, but she didn't like the thought of being inconsiderate.

Sebastian turned the page. "I already ate."

"What?"

He lifted his head up, surprised. "What?"

Naomi nodded. "Yes, that's what I'm asking you. What did you eat?"

It was the first time he looked at a loss for words. "Food."

"You haven't eaten yet. Why not eat now?"

"There's not enough time. I'll eat later." He nodded to her plate. "Your food's getting cold."

"Do you drink coffee?"

He nodded.

"Tea?"

He nodded again.

"Black, white or herbal?"

He frowned, making it clear he didn't realize there was a difference.

"I'm only asking because my mother has invited you over for dinner and to my shame I don't know what you like to eat or drink."

Sebastian snapped his book closed and stared at her. "Your mother's asked me to dinner?"

"Yes."

"With your father there?"

Naomi paused surprised by his question. "Yes," she said slowly, "my father will be there."

"I admire Dr. Mensah very much."

Naomi couldn't help a smile. "It's not like you've kept that a secret." Her father was one topic he couldn't seem to get bored of. He'd told her again about how much her father's London speech had impressed him, how he'd followed his career and read his papers. And he asked about the book her father was working on.

"Have I come on too strong?"

"No," Naomi said, again not quite sure of the question. Did he think she was jealous of her father? It was understandable, he cast a long shadow. "I'm proud of my father's accomplishments. I'm glad you admire them."

Sebastian nodded looking relieved as he pushed her plate towards her as a reminder to eat.

She took a bite of her toast. "And you made an impression on him too because he's the one extending this invitation. My parents are a little annoyed I haven't had them over here for dinner or lunch or anything for that matter."

"Is that what you want? Do you want to host them here? I can—"

"No, no, no. Let my mother do the cooking, it will be a disaster otherwise."

"I can always hire a—"

"No, it's better this way. Unless you don't want to go."

He looked suddenly alarmed. "That's not it. I just—"

"Then answer my question. What do you like to eat? Do you have allergies or any food preferences?"

"No."

Naomi waited for him to expand then realized he wouldn't. "That's it?"

He nodded. "Your mother can make whatever she wants."

"Baked cow tongue? Pickled pig brain? Crispy chicken feet?"

He nodded again. "That's fine."

She was teasing him, but was surprised to see he didn't even wince. Her mother would never serve unfamiliar foods to new guests. "Okay, I'll let her know."

"What time should we be there?"

"Probably around six."

When he frowned, she knew he found her answer too vague. "Six o'clock sharp, but I'll call to make sure."

"What do they like? Wine? Fruit?"

"You don't need to be formal."

"I can't arrive empty handed."

"Flowers."

"What kind?"

"Any kind. It doesn't matter," she said, not realizing that she'd soon regret not being more specific.

Chapter Twelve

A large bouquet of lush peach roses surrounded by pale yellow mini carnations, with bright red Peruvian lilies and luxurious greens greeted them when Naomi and Sebastian entered the Mensah dining room.

"Thank you for the beautiful gift," her mother said, beaming at him as she gestured to a chair. "I'll have to remove it while we're eating, but I wanted you to see it, Dr. Scott."

"Sebastian, please."

"We hope our simple hospitality will warrant such an extravagant gift," her father said, taking a seat at the head of the table.

"The invitation already has."

Mrs. Mensah set out the food and soon the table was filled with the sight of sautéed Maryland crab cakes, the bright red gaze of Ghanaian jollof rice, the scent of grilled asparagus, and spicy cornbread.

Two more guests joined them, the Mensah cats—one white with a patch of black, the other grey. They sat beside Sebastian's chair and stared up at him with matching green eyes.

"Just ignore Julius and Percy," Naomi said. "They're just curious, but they won't jump on you."

"Julius and Percy, huh?" Sebastian looked down at them and nodded.

"Yes, after Julius Richard Petri and Percy Julian," Naomi explained knowing he'd recognize the name of the creator of the Petri dish and the African American research chemist.

He adjusted his glasses. "I don't know what to do with cats."

"You can pet them later," her father said. "They're very polite. But if they bother you—"

"No, no. It's fine," he said and soon they were talking about his work with Naomi.

But it was several minutes into the meal when it became clear that everything wasn't fine.

"Do you not like the food?" Mrs. Mensah asked him.

All eyes went to Sebastian's still empty plate.

"No, it all looks wonderful," he said, glancing down at Percy and Julius who still sat staring up at him.

"Do you want someone to make up a plate for you?" Before he could reply, she nodded to her daughter. "You're closest to him. Give him something."

"No, really I can—"

But Naomi took his plate before he could protest, sending him a glance that it was best not to argue. The cats walked to the other side of his chair.

"More rice," her mother chided. "Do you want him to be as skinny as you?"

"Like that's even possible," Naomi mumbled as she added another large spoonful.

Her father made a low noise of disapproval, making it clear he'd heard her comment.

 She set the now full plate in front of Sebastian. "Enjoy."

"I will."

They waited.

He lifted his fork.

They continued to wait. The cats slowly swished their tails.

Sebastian lifted the fork to his mouth then looked around. "It's delicious."

"You haven't even tasted it yet," Naomi said. "Hurry up." She stiffened her features to mimic a look he usually gave her. "Your food is getting cold."

"Don't rush him," her mother said.

Sebastian took a bite then nodded. "Wonderful." He set his fork down.

"You're not going to finish?"

"I will." He cleared his throat then glanced back down at the cats.

"The cats are making him nervous. Naomi, put them away."

"No, they're fine," Sebastian said, covering Naomi's hand before she could stand, her skin prickled at his touch. "I'm sorry, this is new to me. I usually eat alone." He gestured to their plates. "Just keep talking and eating and pretend that I'm not here."

"That's not how dinner works," Naomi said, half wanting him to remove his hand, half wanting him to leave it there all evening. "You gather with people and talk and eat—together. That's the entire point."

"But if you're feeling awkward," her mother said, "we won't look at you while you eat."

He was no longer just covering her hand; he was absently drawing little circles with his forefinger on the back of her hand. It shouldn't have felt sensuous, but it did. She swallowed and pulled her hand away annoyed at herself and him for making her feel this way. "Mom, that's impossible. Look at the size of him, he's a little hard to ignore."

"Naomi!"

She sent him a firm look. "Eat or I'll feed you myself," she said reminding him of the threat he'd first made when he'd brought the chicken soup.

The corner of his mouth kicked up in a quick grin. "All right," he said, then took another bite. His pace was still slow and a little awkward, but he made his way through the meal until nobody noticed.

At the end of dinner, Naomi and her father sat in the living room and got into a discussion about lymphoproliferation while Mrs. Mensah began to clear the table. Sebastian stood to help her.

"No, I'm fine. Ack, that daughter of mine," she said with a note of frustration and affection as she sent her daughter a look. "She should be helping, but she's oblivious. I blame her father."

"They seem to have a great relationship," he said with a hint of envy.

"They do, heaven help me. What does your father do?"

"He was in the real estate business. He passed away."

"I'm sorry."

"We looked alike, but weren't alike in many ways." He reached for the dishes.

"Please leave me and join them. I can tell that you want to." When she saw him hesitate, she added, "My husband will be disappointed if you don't."

Sebastian tentatively sat down across from Naomi and Dr. Mensah amazed by their easy interaction. His father was bold and loud, while Mr. Mensah was quieter and reserved, but firm in his opinions. His father cared and loved him, but also loved to dictate to him rather than listen. As he grew older their conversations became more stilted, especially when he decided not to follow in his father's footsteps. His father couldn't understand Sebastian's career choice and the distance between them became larger. His father was savvy, bright, but thought the ivory tower of academics was for wimps. Sebastian respected him, but couldn't always relate to him.

Many times Sebastian didn't feel as if he could relate to most people. As a child he'd grown used to eating alone, first because he was in the hospital a lot then at school no one would eat with him, after that he ate alone from the fear of being teased about his size. He remembered in high school one fat girl who only ate salad, loudly complaining that she didn't know why she couldn't lose weight.

He'd wondered the same thing, until he caught her one day sitting alone in a fast food restaurant stuffing her face with cheeseburger and fries like an addict inhaling cocaine. He felt sorry for her and the guilty secret she kept. Another kid, nicknamed The Brick, made eating a performance art. He proudly stacked his tray with everything the cafeteria had to offer that day and consumed everything like a giant sinkhole swallowing up a house.

Sebastian wanted to eat in peace. He didn't want to be like the girl and pretend he didn't know why he was overweight, he liked to eat, it was that simple. But he didn't like people watching and commenting either. Even as he grew and slimmed down a little, he'd gotten into the habit of eating alone, except with his family. Eating with others had become awkward. He didn't feel easy with groups anyway and eating with them only made things worse.

But the Mensahs were different. Once he started eating nobody made a big deal of it. They didn't comment when he took another crab cake or a third helping of cornbread. He realized even Naomi's mention of his size didn't bother him. For some reason, with them he didn't feel sensitive about it.

Sebastian glanced down when he felt something nudge against his leg. He looked at one of the cats, Percy he guessed, and bent down to stroke him. Julius nudged his other leg. Sebastian switched his attention and stroked the cat under his chin. He sat back when he felt he'd petted him enough, but both cats wanted more attention. They jumped up on the couch on either side of him and curled up. He stroked one and then the other until they began to purr.

Sebastian would have spent the remainder of the evening just petting the cats and listening to the conversation, if Dr. Mensah hadn't asked him a direct question about his opinion about natural resistance to infection, which he quickly answered. Naomi disagreed with his response and soon the three were involved in a passionate, heated discussion that lasted until Mrs. Mensah had to interrupt them to announce dessert.

For Sebastian, the evening was a success. Even Naomi seemed amazed by how well he and her parents had gotten on. That night he stared at his reflection in the mirror, hardly recognizing the man who stared back at him. *Keep it together Scott. You're close.*

Phase two of his plan was in place.

But it was no longer all he wanted.

Chapter Thirteen

"Who is that?"

Naomi followed Dr. Vera Conklin's cool hazel gaze to where Sebastian sat in the small café. Few things could escape the older woman whose crisp dark suit emphasized her boxy frame. Her sun-washed, blonde hair with streaks of grey was pulled back from her face in a bun and clear framed glasses gave her the appearance of the brilliant woman she was. She'd gotten her doctorate in cell biology and with her former husband, Niklaas, was known in the field for her research into bacterial infections such as listeria. Naomi had asked to meet her mentor for lunch and although she'd given Sebastian the day off, he'd decided to stay three tables away. "He's my new personal assistant."

"I didn't know you needed an assistant."

"Neither did I until he showed up. He's better than he looks."

"Couldn't you have found someone a little more…" She waved her hand searching for words.

"I didn't find him. He found me. It's a long story. Just pretend he's not there."

"That's impossible. He's quite unforgettable. I couldn't believe it when I saw you two coming in together. The way he held the door open for you was almost medieval."

"He's not that bad," Naomi said feeling a little defensive. He was being courteous not medieval. Was it wrong for him to hold the door open for her? And he was hard to ignore, even more so than before. His appearance wasn't as shabby as it had been in the past and he'd gotten his hair cut and his beard trimmed. When had that happened and why hadn't she noticed it sooner? She wasn't the only one to notice his improved appearance, catching the waitress sneaking glances at him.

"I didn't want to say anything," Vera said with a note of caution. "But he looks a little bit like Sebastian Scott."

"Probably because he is."

She stared at Naomi wide-eyed for a few seconds then closed her mouth and shook her head. "Get rid of him immediately."

"You think I haven't tried?" Naomi said with a laugh, even though she didn't want him to leave anymore.

"He can't be on your project."

"He's not."

"What if people find out?"

"How would they? I won't get my funding yanked because of a personal relationship."

"How personal is it?"

"I just told you. He's my assistant. Nothing more." Although she had imagined what it would be like if it became something more, especially that one night only a week after he'd had dinner at her parents, when she'd gone downstairs for a late night snack and found him lying face up on the kitchen floor…

"Oh my God," she cried, racing over to him. "Sebastian, are you okay?" She felt for a pulse.

She heard him mumble something.

"What? Where are you hurt?"

"Stay away from me," he said. "I'm a little drunk."

He was splayed on the cold kitchen floor wearing only his dark blue pajama bottoms. She could guess that he was more than a little drunk, even though she didn't smell much alcohol on him. Was he really that much of a lightweight when it came to drinking?

"Come on," she said. "Let me help you up."

He didn't move. "I don't think I can keep this up. I can't do it anymore."

He was ready to quit? Had she worked him too hard? A part of her heart lifted, then fell and she faced the terrible truth—she didn't want him to.

"You just need to rest," she said, struggling to lift him up. His skin felt hot beneath her fingers and soon her nightgown felt like a flimsy barrier between him and her own nakedness. He fell back against her, his back resting on her breasts, the heat from his skin seeping through the cotton fabric.

"Naomi, I—"

She didn't want to hear him say he wanted to quit. "Don't say anything you'll regret." She tried to push him forward, biting her lip when she felt the urge to press her mouth against the expanse of his back and shoulders.

He sighed then straightened, moving away from her. "I'm sorry." He turned to her, his compelling brown eyes holding her still. "I didn't mean to scare you."

He didn't scare her. He made her heart pound, her hands tremble, her blood rush. She wanted to feel his skin next to hers. She wanted to feel his lips pressed against hers again, but this time deeper and longer. And he didn't seem drunk—he looked sexy and sober. Or was that just her imagination? She hugged herself to keep herself still. "Are you sure you're not hurt?"

"I'm sure. I do that sometimes. I get hot and like the feel of the cool tiles against my back."

His back. His beautiful, broad back. Oh to be the tiles on the kitchen floor.

Sebastian rose to his feet then held his hand out to lift her up. She didn't move, continuing to stare up at him. "You've lost weight." He'd always been big, but over the past few weeks he'd become more toned and with his shirt off it was easy to notice.

"Hmm."

He lifted up the muffin and saw she'd scrawled her number on a napkin underneath. He looked at her and saw her watching him. He smiled back, tucking her number inside his jacket pocket so as not to hurt her feelings.

He glanced at Naomi who was having an intense conversation, she probably hadn't even noticed. He had to stop watching her. He had to stop thinking about her.

He pulled out his cell phone and read some news then paused when he heard high heels stop at his table. He looked up and saw an attractive woman in leopard patterned heels, form fitting black dress with a spicy, floral scent. "Could you tell me where the Trust Bank is?"

Sebastian stood and gave her directions, patiently answering questions she could have figured out on her own.

"That sounds complicated," she finally said. "Do you think you could show me?"

He sat back down. "Umm…I'm waiting for someone."

She looked disappointed then placed her card on the table and slid it towards him. "In case they don't show up."

He plastered on a smile, confused. What kind of coffee shop was this? He'd never gotten this kind of attention before. Even at the height of his career, most women looked past him. He glanced down at his shirt. Was it the new clothes? Andre had forced him into dark trousers and a casual dark blue crew neck he'd never tried before and the light rimmed frames were new for him too.

He heard the chair in front of him scrape across the ground and tensed. Was it another woman wanting something? Would she ask him the time or the best place to buy seafood?

He glanced up when he heard a fingernail tap against the table. His tension eased when he saw Naomi.

"Why were you looking down like that?"

Sebastian leaned forward and lowered his voice. "I don't know what's going on. Two women have given me their phone numbers."

"That's no surprise. You're a good looking man."

"Would you give me your number?"

She laughed. "You already have it."

"I mean, if you didn't know me."

She shook her head.

He felt his heart fall.

"I'd feel too shy," she said. "I wouldn't have the boldness."

His heart lifted. Maybe if he played this right, there was a chance… "Naomi—"

She rested her chin in her hand. "I really like these," she said, tapping the frames of her own glasses. "You look more approachable than before."

Approachable? That wasn't exactly a come on. He didn't know what to say so he started to stand.

She covered his hand with hers, stopping him. "We're not leaving yet. There's something I have to say."

He slowly sat back down, his heart racing. She was touching him and looking at him in a way she never had before. Did she feel the attraction too? Did she feel conflicted because he worked for her?

"I want to help you."

His heart fell to the floor and cracked. He'd built up his hopes for nothing. He adjusted his frames, trying to look nonchalant. "W-what?"

"I think I've finally figured out why you wanted to volunteer with me."

Sebastian froze. Did she really know? Could this be the moment he'd been waiting for?

To his relief and regret she pulled her hand away and folded her arms looking pleased with herself. "You want me to find out what really happened with your research."

He felt his throat tighten. This was not good. "I made an error, that's all. I didn't—"

Naomi shook her head, cutting him off. "But you're not the type. You're very fastidious. Over the last couple of months I see how you think. I can see why you rose so fast. Besides, we both know you can't work with me like this forever."

"I like what I do," he said in a hard tone. He didn't want her looking into his past.

"Don't you want more?"

"It's a dead end. Focus on your career."

"You may not know this, but Dr. Vera Conklin is the wife of—"

"Dr. Niklaas Conklin the head researcher at BioCorps, yes I know. Did you talk to her about me?"

"Yes, I thought she could help us—"

"What did she say?"

Naomi hesitated then sighed. "That I should leave it alone."

"Listen to her and never mention this again." He stood. "Are you ready to leave?"

He steeled himself against the look of disappointment on her face. He wouldn't weaken, he couldn't change the past. He looked at the window just as Vera passed, briefly catching her eye and the silent message there.

He had to go forward with his plan fast before Naomi ruined everything.

Chapter Fifteen

She hadn't meant to make him angry, Naomi thought as she headed up the driveway after a long walk, her skin feeling sticky from the humid air.

For the past week, Sebastian kept their interactions brief. He talked about her father and the lab. That was it. She was going to lose him and she didn't want that.

She didn't want to hurt him, but something about Vera's tone and Sebastian's reaction bothered her. She didn't know why yet. She didn't see the harm in making some simple inquiries into the BioCorps incident. She got her hands on as much public information as possible, but she knew she would need to get more.

Naomi paused when she saw Josephine sitting in the garden, reading a book, a glass of lemonade on the white table beside her. They only nodded greetings to each other, but never spoke. Although she no longer leaned as heavily on her cane as she used to, she made no move to leave and still glanced at Naomi with a look of suspicion. But Naomi wanted to help Sebastian; to know more about him. Josephine was somebody who could help her.

"It's a lovely day," Naomi said, walking up to her.

"Yes," Josephine said, not looking up. "What ridiculous errand are you going to send my son on this week?"

She deserved that, although she'd stopped with that petty revenge weeks ago. "He's a very hard worker."

"That's the problem. My son shouldn't be working. At least not like this. He and his brother inherited a lucrative business from their father. There's no reason he's doing this."

Naomi sat in the other garden chair. "I agree and I'd like to help him."

For a moment, Josephine's face lit up and her eyes softened. "How?"

"I know he's meant for more. He's got a brilliant mind and he could do so much in the field of research."

Josephine's face hardened. "It broke his heart already. I won't see him hurt again. If you truly want to help my son, you'll help him come to his senses."

Naomi inwardly winced at the way Josephine said 'my son' as if Sebastian were a possession or pet she meant to keep close by.

"I don't think he's out of his mind, Mrs. Scott, but that he's searching for something and—"

A cruel smile spread on Josephine face. "Don't delude yourself into thinking you can help him find it."

"I don't."

"Many women think that Sebastian's like other men."

"I would never—"

Josephine closed her book and rested it on her lap. "My husband was the same way. Oh you should have seen the way the women flocked to him. They all thought they were the one for him. Only I knew what he needed. I was—"

"I don't think you know what your son needs."

Josephine grabbed her glass and tossed her lemonade in Naomi's face. "Don't you dare tell me what I know."

Naomi brushed the ice cubes from her lap and wiped her eyes, the cold drink soaking her blouse and stinging her eyes. "I didn't mean—"

"You're an arrogant, stupid woman if you think you know more about him than I do."

Naomi licked her lips, tasting the tart juice on her mouth. "Mrs. Scott I—I only wanted to help Sebastian find his way back to a career he clearly loves."

"And I'm letting you know that he loves his family and his business. The business his father gave to him to keep and pass on for generations to come."

"But if he doesn't want—"

"This isn't about Sebastian, this is what you want. Your selfish desires to trap him back in a life that doesn't suit him. If you have a heart at all, you'll see that." She stood and marched away.

For a moment she'd been fooled. Josephine hated being fooled. If only that Mensah woman had wanted to help Sebastian for the right reasons. She likely wanted to use him to advance her career just like Barbara had. Although his reputation was in shambles, she knew he was brilliant. Why did her son have to be so blind to these ambitious women?

But at least this one didn't pretend to be interested in him as a man. But was she really unaware of the effect she had on Sebastian. Did she pretend not to see the change in him? Or was that all an act?

Josephine marched through the French doors into the cool solarium and took a seat.

She'd lied to Naomi. Sebastian was nothing like his father—a charismatic, boisterous man who could light up a room. Neither of her sons had her husband's ability to both charm and make money. They had those attributes split into two. Gregg could charm; Sebastian could make money. They needed each other and the business needed them both or it would fall apart. Sebastian had to stay and run the company that had been his father's dream.

She still remembered the look on her husband's face when he'd first held Sebastian in the hospital. "He's going to carry on my legacy," he'd said. "My father handed me nothing, but I'm giving this boy the world. He won't have to struggle as I had. He'll take the reins of my company and make it even greater than it is now."

Josephine blinked back tears at the memory. She and her husband had both come from families that had nothing to pass down—except hard work and poverty. Josephine had always dreamed of being part of something bigger.

She'd envied those who could trace their roots back generations with a level of pride she could never share. Her husband had come from a small island with nothing, but had made a big impact due to his brains and drive. He'd built a business that could sustain them for generations. Was it wrong to make her sons hold onto something she'd never had? Something their father had never had? Sebastian had to fulfill the destiny his father had set for him, or all his efforts meant nothing.

If only she knew what Sebastian needed from Naomi. That was the key to untangling the chain she held around him. Josephine gripped her hands around the arm of the white chair. She felt that she was slowly losing him and losing him would be like losing her husband all over again. She couldn't bare that.

She saw Andre passing by and called out to him.

"Yes?" he said, standing in the entryway.

"I need another glass of lemonade. I spilled the last one in the garden," she said, making a vague gesture to it.

He nodded. "Are you sure you haven't gotten too much sun? You look…upset."

"Have you found out anything more about Naomi?"

"Nothing more than I told you. I don't think there's anything to worry about. She seems to be good for him."

The woman even had Andre fooled. "I'm not too sure about that."

"Why not? He's like his old self again."

Josephine gripped one hand into a fist. She couldn't admit that that scared her the most.

Chapter Sixteen

Sebastian stared at his cell phone. It was now or never. He had to make the first move to finalize his plan. He started to dial.

"I thought you said you weren't going to hurt her," Andre demanded, storming into Sebastian's study, startling him.

He dropped the phone and swore. He bent down and picked up the phone, glad it was protected in its case. "What is wrong with you?"

Andre jumped in front of him and waved a napkin in his face. "What is this?"

"It looks like a napkin to me. What do you think it is?"

Andre held the napkin between his hands. "I mean this."

Sebastian read the waitress's scrawled phone number. "It's a number."

"I thought I told you not to hurt her."

"I'm not hurting anyone."

"Do you think I helped you so you could pick up other women?"

"I didn't change for her."

When Andre sent him a knowing look he said, "Listen, it wasn't supposed to be like this. You're right. At first I did want to use her. I wanted to use her to get close to her father. I heard he was writing a book and I wanted to help him with the research, but I knew if he knew who I was he wouldn't give me a chance. So I came up with the idea of getting close to his daughter instead. I thought if I got on her good side and he saw what I did; he couldn't help but want to work with me." After hearing Dr. Mensah's lecture in London, Sebastian had kept tabs on him and knew what the proposed book was about, he'd also learned how Dr. Mensah was using his own time and funds to do extensive research. Sebastian knew with his resources he could take Dr. Mensah's project to an entirely different level and by collaborating with Dr. Mensah he would get his name seen in a good light again. "Working with her father was to be my redemption." Sebastian saw Andre's face change and dread slowly covered his heart. He lowered his voice. "Naomi's standing behind me right now, isn't she?"

Andre nodded.

"How close?"

"Close enough."

Sebastian sighed and turned around. "Naomi."

She held out a book to him, her expression neutral. "You said you wanted to read it." She spun away.

He followed her. "Let me explain."

"You just did." She slapped her forehead with the palm of her hand. "How could I have been stupid enough to think you really wanted to work with me?" She shook her head. "Don't worry, you're not the first. I'm a human stepping stone. Monica wanted to work with Pete. Barry preferred to marry my sister." She stopped walking and faced him. "And you…you prefer to work with my father. Fine, I'll put in a good word for you. You'll get the job. We can end this charade now." She headed for her room.

"Naomi—"

"Do I get to keep the lab?"

"Of course."

"Good. I'll start looking for somewhere else to live."

"You don't need to do that." He grabbed her wrist and spun her to him. "Listen, I know I should have been honest from the beginning—"

"Why?" she shot back as tears gathered in her eyes. "That would have defeated your purpose."

"I do enjoy working for you."

"Really? Is that why I found you on the kitchen floor, telling me that you wanted to quit?"

"I didn't say that."

"You said, 'I can't do it anymore.'"

Sebastian shook his head. "That's not what I meant. I—"

She took off her glasses and wiped the tears from her eyes. "I'm such a fool! Why would you want to work with me when you have my father?"

"Naomi," he said softly, her name like a plea on his lips.

"Now everything makes sense." She turned away from him as if the sight of him pained her. "Why you were so eager to impress my parents with the large bouquet. Why you mentioned my father's research every chance you got." She shifted her gaze back to his face, her eyes red but defiant. "You think I don't know how unhappy you've been lately? You've hardly spoken to me these last few weeks."

He sighed heavily, his voice filled with regret. "Naomi, it's not what you think—"

"Do you want to work with my father?"

"Yes, but—"

"Then I'll make it happen." She spun away. "I'm going to change and go to the lab. I have some work I want to do." She sent him a cold glance over her shoulder. "Alone."

Chapter Seventeen

Josephine only hated listening to one of the voices on the other ended of the phone, the other was calmer and less prone to panic, but she wasn't surprised by the call. It was bound to happen. She spoke in a low voice as she sat in her bedroom. "You didn't have to call me."

"This shouldn't have happened," the calm voice demanded. "Tell me what went wrong."

"Nothing."

"She has to be stopped," the panicked voice said.

The first voice spoke. "There's nothing to find."

"But what if—"

"She's nobody, there's nothing to worry about."

"If she keeps digging she'll find something."

"What do you want me to do?" Josephine asked, tired of being in between their argument.

"He must have mentioned something," Calm Voice said.

"Sebastian keeps his promises," Josephine said, offended. "This is all her. I knew she was trouble."

"Why is he working with her?"

"I don't know."

"We had a deal."

"I know that," Josephine said in a tight voice.

"If you want us to trust you, you know what to do. We all have something to lose."

The line went dead.

Chapter Eighteen

Her father? Her father! All this time Sebastian really wanted to work with her father! How could she have been so stupid? Naomi burned with humiliation as she looked at the samples in her lab.

Stupid. Stupid. Stupid. All the signs had been there, even from the first meeting. The moment he'd seen her father, his expression changed and he'd gushed about her father's lecture. And when he'd brought up her father's work and accomplishments, she'd foolishly thought he was trying to impress her with his knowledge.

The haircut and new clothes had probably been for her father's sake too.

That's why Sebastian had gotten sullen after meeting with her parents. He had gotten bored with her and was eager to pass her by and head to his true goal: the great Abraham Mensah. That's why he had no interest in her helping him with the BioCorps scandal. He had no interest in her.

When she'd broken up with Barry and he'd turned his attention to her sister, it hadn't hurt at all. Not even a twinge. She liked him, but only as a friend. She truly felt happy for her sister. But her father made her feel jealous. Jealous that he'd soon get to spend time with Sebastian and laugh and discuss topics of interest. She'd come to enjoy his company and she liked him. Very much.

Naomi closed her eyes against gathering tears. She took a deep breath.

Work. She'd focus on work. She was in her favorite place, doing her favorite thing. She didn't need a man like Sebastian. She didn't need any man.

She worked until the next morning, feeling tired and bleary eyed by the time it was close to the arrival of the first researcher of the team. She'd go home and take a quick nap then return in the afternoon. Naomi opened the front door to her lab and gasped when she saw Sebastian standing there.

He didn't say a word, but his expression said "We need to talk" and she knew he wouldn't let her escape him.

Chapter Nineteen

He led her outside, holding onto her arm as if afraid she'd run away. "I want you to listen to me carefully," he said. "I did—do want to work with your father, but that's not the only thing I want—-shit!"

Naomi looked up at him startled, when he suddenly spun them in the other direction. Before she could ask him what was wrong a female voice called out to him.

"Sebastian? Sebastian is that you?"

He groaned and increased his pace. Clearly he wanted to avoid the other woman, but Naomi wasn't in the mood to let him. His shaggy appearance in the past had likely been part of his ploy to get her to pity him. He actually pretended to be surprised in the coffee shop about the women's attention when he was likely used to it. No man could be that clueless to his own appeal.

His mother had told her that he'd inherited his father's successful business; there had likely been plenty of women who'd wanted to get close to him before. She'd stopped herself from being one of them. She was relieved she'd never revealed her feelings; he would have felt sorry for her. She glanced back at the woman and saw she was attractive with cupid bow lips and hair sculpted in a sleek look.

Naomi stopped walking. "Someone appears to be calling you."

"No," he tugged her forward. "It's not like that."

She yanked her arm free. "I'd hate to get in the way of one of your ladies."

He pressed his hands together, his eyes pleading. "Naomi, please let me—"

"Sebastian Scott?" the woman asked, peering up at him when he lowered his head.

He sighed and lifted his head, forcing a smile. "Yes."

She playfully slapped him on the arm. "I thought it was you!" She playfully slapped him again and giggled. "You haven't changed. Well, except for the wheelchair. I'm not used to looking up at you like this. You look great."

He shoved his hands in his pockets. "You too." He turned to Naomi. "This is Dr. Naomi Mensah. Naomi, Molly Robb."

Molly shook Naomi's hand. "Doctor, huh? I've been looking for a new GP. They're so hard to find nowadays."

"I'm afraid I'm not that kind of doctor," Naomi said.

"Oh," Molly said disappointed then smiled again. "So, what did he tell you about me?" She grimaced. "Poor Sebastian. We were so vicious to you back then. Sometimes I can't believe how mean I was. But I guess kids will be kids, right?"

He shrugged nonchalant.

Naomi didn't feel the same way. She didn't like Molly's arrogance that Sebastian would have told her about Molly or the way Molly was looking at him with a superficial embarrassment for her past behavior. Naomi hadn't been around other kids her age long enough to get teased or was too oblivious to notice. She felt a little guilty for forcing Sebastian to face a woman who clearly made him feel uncomfortable. Although she was mad at him, she didn't want him punished like this.

She leaned forward. "I'm sorry, what was your name again?"

"Molly Robb."

"And where did you know each other from?"

"Middle and high school."

Naomi nodded and laughed. "Oh, maybe that's why he's never mentioned you before. I was trying to place you and I just couldn't but now it all makes sense." Naomi linked her arm through his. "It was so long ago and unimportant."

Molly's gaze hardened. "I heard about BioCorps." She made a face. "Poor Sebastian, I read all about it."

"Yes, read and likely didn't understand half of it. The paper can only put so much in layman's terms." Naomi pulled out her phone and squeezed closer to him. "Darling, we'll be late."

Sebastian stiffened whether at the affectionate term or her closeness, Naomi didn't know, but he quickly played along, unlocking their arms and wrapping his around her shoulders. "Right, bye Molly. Like my wife said, it's all forgotten."

It was now Naomi's turn to stiffen in surprise. *Wife?! She was playing his girlfriend.*

Sebastian turned them away from Molly and they walked several steps in silence, Naomi feeling like a tiny sparrow taking shade under a massive oak tree. She'd walked close to him before, but never like this, feeling the warmth and weight of his arm around her shoulders. It felt good. Too good. She had to remember he'd used her.

Naomi looked back. "She's gone." She began to pull away, but he didn't let her. "We don't have to pretend anymore." She released a laugh. "I'm still angry at you, but there was something about the way that woman was talking to you that annoyed me and the nasty tone she used when she mentioned you being in a wheelchair just—"

She stopped when she caught a glimpse of herself in the reflection of a shop window. She looked like a mad scientist! Her hair was springing out of its braid, one collar on her shirt stood up while the other was down, even her glasses were slightly askew. Normally she didn't care, especially after spending all night in the lab, but remembering the sight of Molly's sophisticated appearance she was stunned the other woman didn't laugh in her face. You? His wife? No way.

She straightened and pushed up her glasses. "I can't believe you didn't tell me I looked like this. You—"

Sebastian didn't let her finish. He pulled her into an alley between two buildings, put his arms around her and kissed her. The touch of his lips sent her stomach into a wild swirl, and she reveled in his warm embrace while his slow, soft kiss melted her anger away.

When he finally drew away, his brown eyes studied her face as if in wonder. "That was Molly Robb," he said his hoarse voice barely a whisper.

"I-I know," Naomi stammered, her heart racing so fast she could hardly breathe. She stared up at him stunned. "I'm sorry."

He gently cupped her face in his large hands and kissed her again. "You stood up to Molly Robb for me." He smoothed down her hair, then brushed his knuckles against her cheek, his voice deepening with emotion. "You beautiful, wonderful..." He kissed her again. And again.

Naomi didn't move, not wanting it to end even though she didn't know what was happening.

"No one has ever stood up for me like that," he said, his breath warm against her lips.

"I didn't really do anything," she said unsure.

He rested his hands on the wall behind her, trapping her in the circle of his arms, a sly smile tugging at his mouth. "That was Molly Robb."

"So you've said."

"She made my life hell in middle school. There may still even be a clip of it online. She always loomed so large in my mind, but you made her look so small."

Naomi glanced at the size of one of his arms, positioned near her head. "Compared to you, she is small." She looked up at him perplexed. "Don't you realize how attractive you are?"

He lowered his head embarrassed. "I wish you'd stop saying that."

"I'm not flattering you, it's true." She ducked under one of his arms, feeling her anger returning. She was ready to leave.

He grabbed the back of her shirt, and pulled her back in place, lowering his arm so that it was shoulder level. "It wasn't always true. I was an overweight kid in a wheelchair for many years, then I was a nerd with a rich dad. I don't think anyone's ever found me attractive." A slow smile spread on his face. "Until now."

She turned her face when he bent to kiss her. "I'm sure you just didn't notice."

He pressed his lips against the curve of her neck. "I would have noticed," he mumbled

She pushed him away, determined not to weaken. He could make her knees weak, but only a few hours ago he'd made her cry. "I'm still mad at you."

"I know. I'm sorry." He sighed. "If you don't want me to work with your father, I won't."

She knew how much that admission cost him. She could see in his eyes how much he wanted to. "But you still want to."

He straightened, shoving his hands in his pockets. "Yes."

"Then I'll talk to him," she said, although she'd miss him as her assistant. She knew it had all been too good to be true. "I don't like your methods, but I understand your ambition. There's nothing wrong with going after what you want."

His eyes caught and held hers. "Is there anything wrong with wanting to sleep with you tonight?"

Chapter Twenty

"And you ran away?" Elia said when Naomi told her what had happened.

The two sisters sat in the backyard watching Elia's daughter Susan slide down her play set.

"I didn't know what else to do."

"Given him a date and a time?"

"I panicked."

"What's to panic about? You've been working together for months."

"Working not dating."

"It's been 'Sebastian this' and 'Sebastian that' for weeks."

"I don't sound like that."

"This is the first time you mentioned a man's name without also using microbe inspired gobblygook."

"It's not gobblygook."

"Why did you run?"

Naomi took off her glasses and rubbed her eyes. "Because I needed to get away from him."

"You live in the same house."

Naomi shoved her glasses back on and threw up her hands. "I know!"

"Know what?" Barry asked, coming through the glass doors, having put their younger daughter down for a nap.

"Nothing," Naomi said, sending her sister a look of warning.

"We're just talking about men."

He held out his arms. "I'm an expert, if you need any advice."

"I don't." Naomi nodded towards her niece. "Looks like she wants to be pushed on the swing." Presently Susan was hanging upside down on the jungle gym, but Barry took the hint and went to play with his daughter.

Elia took a deep breath. "I don't understand this. Why do you need to get away from him?"

"Because I'm confused. He's confusing me. I don't know what he wants."

"He's made it quite clear what he wants."

"It doesn't make sense. One moment he wants to use me so that he can work with Dad, the next he wants…you know."

"Sex isn't a dirty word or act." She winked. "Unless you want it to be."

Naomi folded her arms. "I'm going to have to move again." She rested her head back and groaned. "I'll probably have to stay with Mom and Dad until I can find a place."

"If we didn't have guests coming soon, you know we would—"

Naomi stared up at the sky, watching a plane fly overhead. "I know you'd let me stay here."

"But I don't think you have to move."

She sat up. "I'm not going to be used again." She shook her head. "Not like this. I feel like he's getting a two for one bargain."

Elia folded her arms. "So what?"

Naomi's mouth fell open. "So *what?*"

"Yes, so he likes you and Dad. So he wants to work with Dad and be with you, what's the big deal?"

"The big deal is he's changed so much since the first time I met him that I don't feel like I know who he is. Would you risk your heart on a man like that?"

"So you're in love with him, then?"

"Will you stick to the point?"

"The point is you've got a man you're attracted to who wants to sleep with you and you run to your younger sister like a scardy cat."

"All right I admit it. I'm scared. I'm terrified because I do care about him and I don't want to get hurt."

"But that's not what life's about. You can't hide in your lab forever. You can't stay safe in a neat, sterile environment forever. Life is messy, but it's also wonderful. Didn't you once tell me that you loved science because it was about asking questions and seeking the answers? You said you didn't care if you failed. It was the adventure of experimenting that thrilled you. Love is the same." Elia shook her head in regret. "I don't have all the answers and I don't know him well, but I do know that since you've met him you've been happy in a way I've never seen before."

Her cell phone rang. Naomi looked at the number and froze. "It's him."

"Answer it," Elia said.

"But it's him."

Elia rolled her eyes. "I know. You're lucky he didn't call you right away. Have you forgotten? You ran away from him."

Naomi shook her head. "I can't talk to him."

Her sister reached for the phone. "I can."

Naomi held it out of reach. "But you're not going to."

"You need to talk to him."

"I'll talk to him when I'm ready."

The phone stopped ringing.

"You just lost your chance," Elia said with a sigh. "You could have had a lovely evening instead you're stuck here with me."

The phone alerted her to a text.

She read it. "That's strange."

Elia leaned over to see. "What?"

"He's inviting me to go swimming."

"Say yes."

She hesitated. "But it's not like him to—"

"Naomi, don't over think this. This is your chance. Don't blow it."

Her sister was right. She wouldn't run away again, she did want to see him. She had to face life and all its mysteries. Love was something new to discover. She typed in her reply and hit Send.

Chapter Twenty-one

Gregg Scott stared at his older brother who sat across from him in the fast causal restaurant. They'd decided to stop at the American grill type facility for lunch after looking at one of their proper-ties. "Got something on your mind?" he asked as one of the waiters walked past their table with a hot pan of sizzling meat, filled with the scent of jalapeno peppers.

"No, why?"

Gregg nodded to his brother's cup. "Because you just put pepper in your coffee."

Sebastian looked down and swore.

"I know meeting me to look at the Renton property wasn't on your schedule but—"

"It's not that," Sebastian said, lifting his hand to get the attention of one of the wait staff. "I need another coffee," he said when a fresh faced teenager with six earrings approached.

"What is it then?"

"I made a mistake."

"What kind of mistake?"

"With a woman."

"Don't worry," Gregg said with a laugh. "We all make those."

Sebastian thanked the waitress when she set down his coffee and reached for the sugar. "I thought that being honest would fix things, but I think I made things worse."

"What did you say?"

"When should you tell a woman you want to sleep with her?"

Gregg stared at him. "You told a woman you wanted to sleep with her?"

"Yes."

"Just like that?"

"Yes."

His mouth fell open. "Are you out of your mind?"

"Clearly."

"Who is she?"

He hesitated.

Gregg read the expression on his brother's face and groaned. "Don't tell me it's Naomi Mensah." When his brother didn't reply, he swore. "You're lucky you're not really employed or she could sue you for harassment or something."

"I thought she wanted it too."

"What did she do when you said it? Did she slap you?"

Sebastian took a sip of his coffee. "Forget I said anything."

"No way. What did she do?"

Sebastian took another sip then set his cup down. "She ran away."

Gregg looked at him for a long moment then threw his head back and laughed.

Sebastian frowned. "It's not funny."

"How old is she? Fifteen?" He laughed harder.

Sebastian lowered his gaze and slowly turned his cup counter clockwise. "I'll make you stop laughing in a minute."

Gregg quickly sobered. "I'm sorry."

Sebastian lifted his coffee.

"It's just…" Gregg started to laugh again, then quickly covered it with a cough. "I want to help."

"You can't help. I have to find a way to fix this."

"There's no way. You already put it out there. It's like trying to unring a bell. You should have waited until you were more certain of her."

"I know that now."

"Give her time. How long has it been?"

"It happened this morning. She won't return my calls."

"It's not like you don't know where she lives."

That didn't make things any easier. First he'd blundered by letting her overhear that he'd initially used her so that he could get to work with her father and now he'd told her how he'd felt and been rejected. He should have kept his mouth shut. Now he could lose two things he'd wanted.

He returned home that late afternoon in a foul mood.

Andre met him at the door. "What are you doing here?"

Sebastian closed the door behind him. "I live here."

"B-but I thought you were meeting with Naomi."

"Why?"

"I just saw her about fifteen minutes ago. She told me she was meeting you to go swimming. She looked very eager."

"Swimming?"

"Yes, you sent her a text."

Sebastian felt his heart sink to his stomach. "I didn't send her a text." And Naomi couldn't swim.

Chapter Twenty-two

He found her floating face down in the water.

Sheer, stark terror raced through him. *How could this have happened?* She couldn't be dead. He dove in the water and pulled her out, while Andre called an ambulance.

"Come on Naomi," Sebastian pleaded doing chest compressions on her limp, lifeless body. "Naomi, you came here to meet me and I'm here now. You can't leave me again. Come on, Naomi you can fight this. You're not going to die on me."

But she didn't move, there was no flicker of life left in her.

Please, please, please, he silently prayed. She'd come to him. She'd wanted to see him. To give him a second chance after running away. He couldn't lose her, not like this.

"Let me take over," Andre said.

Sebastian gritted his teeth. "No," he said, continuing to do the steady compressions, until he feared he'd break her ribs. Soon despair swallowed his hope, if she didn't breathe soon her brain would be affected. Just as the crucial time ticked close, she vomited up water. He turned her head and she took a long gasp.

He gathered her in his arms, holding her close, more for his sake than for hers. He needed to feel her body close to his, to feel her cold skin grow warm in his embrace and be certain that she was protected, that nothing could get past him. "It's okay," he said gently. "You're safe now. You're going to be all right."

It was all still a blur.

Naomi lay in the hospital bed still trying to understand how she'd ended up there.

She remembered getting Sebastian's text and feeling both anxious and eager to see him again. Her sister had helped her purchase a new suit and swim cap and on the drive there, she practiced what she'd planned to say to him. Was swimming supposed to be foreplay? Did he still want to spend the night with her? She wasn't going to run away this time. If she didn't learn how to swim that night, it would be fine with her.

Then he hadn't been at the pool, which confused her because Sebastian was usually prompt. After that she couldn't remember much else except, hearing echoing footsteps, which she thought was odd since she'd expected him to be barefoot, and then she felt a hard shove at the base of her back.

She hit the water with a splash, panic and fear seizing her as she fought to keep her head above water. Blackness soon followed. The next thing she remembered was Sebastian holding her then being whisked into an ambulance.

Naomi reached for her glasses and saw a figure in the corner. She was about to scream when the figure spoke. "It's me," Sebastian said. "You're safe." He stood and came out of the shadows. "You'll be discharged soon."

"Good."

"You don't remember what happened?"

I have my suspicions, but not enough to share. "Not really. I think I slipped."

Sebastian stood beside her bed, his dark gaze holding hers. "Are you ready to tell me what you've been up to?"

"I don't know what you mean?"

He took her hand and sat on the side of the bed. "Then let me be clearer. Give me a reason why someone would want to kill you."

Chapter Twenty-three

"Kill me?" her voice cracked in surprise. "Who would want to kill me?"

"That's what I want to know. How much should the police know?"

"Know about what?"

"Whatever you're not telling me."

"There's no need for the police. Do you think I'm involved in something illegal?"

"No."

Naomi rubbed her forehead. "This is all so strange. I thought that after...I ran off...you'd forgiven me by offering to give me lessons."

"I didn't text you."

Her face burned, she lowered her head embarrassed. Someone had made a fool of her. "Oh."

"I wish I had."

Her head shot up. "Really?"

"Yes," his jaw twitched. "Then this might not have happened. Do you think any of the men that showed up at your former apartment had a grudge? Did you tell someone to get lost in a way that might have made him angry?"

"Yes, but it's been months since then."

Sebastian fell silent then said, "You're hiding something from me."

Yes. "No, I'm not. You know everything about my schedule. I don't have room for any secrets. Unlike some," she said, reminding him of the real reason he'd approached her.

"We're not talking about your father right now. Why did someone attack you?"

"How do you know someone attacked me? I said I slipped—"

"And I said, I didn't send you a text. Now answer my question. Why would someone attack you?"

"I don't know," she said honestly. "I haven't been doing anything except…" She stopped as a thought came to her.

His gaze darkened. "Except what?"

She rested her head back. "I'm sure it's nothing."

"What?"

"I know you hate talking about the past."

"Go on."

"I was looking into the BioCorps case." She held up her hand before he could speak. "But I haven't found anything so I don't see how the two could be connected."

Sebastian's gaze hardened as did his voice. "I told you to leave it alone."

"I was just…I wanted to help. What if it was sabotage? Internal espionage? Maybe you could be vindicated."

He sighed. "Are you really this naïve?"

"What?"

"Do you think I wouldn't have thought about that? Do you think these past five years I wouldn't have looked at this from many different angles?"

"But I thought with fresh new eyes I could—"

"What?" he said with a sneer. "Restore me to my former glory? Do you have any idea how big this case is?"

"That doesn't frighten me."

"It should and I hope it does now."

Naomi folded her arms. "It makes me angry. If someone tried to hurt me then I'm on the right track."

He stood and looked out the window. "They didn't try to hurt you, they tried to *kill* you. Make an effort to understand the difference."

"A moment of desperation. You must see what we have here."

"I mean it. Let it go."

"You can't walk away from this."

Sebastian spun around with anger in his eyes. "Yes, I can. I have. I can't restore my reputation. I made a choice and I have to live with the consequences. I once got my hopes up that I could…" He shook his head in frustration. "It's too late for me."

"If you had hope once you can have it again. You were alone before. This time I can—"

"No."

"But I believe in you. If we can prove—"

"I said no. Leave this alone. Am I clear?"

"Isn't it worse not knowing?"

Sebastian shook his head and tapped his chest. "I *know* what happened. End of story. I like what I do and now I just—"

"Want to work with my father," Naomi finished in a dry tone. "I get it."

"Do you want me to leave?"

Her voice cracked in surprise. "No."

He pointed at her. "Then stop playing games."

"I'm not."

"Someone tried to kill you and you want me to focus on rebuilding my reputation? Right now all I can think about is how to find the bastard who did this to you and tear him into pieces. Yes, I want to work with your father, but I love you."

Naomi hung her head, trying to process his words. *He loved her?* What did that mean? She knew he wanted to sleep with her, she could accept him liking her, but love? The big L.O.V.E? Would it be wise to believe him or was it another strategy to manipulate her? But he looked genuinely upset as if she meant a lot to him. "I'm sorry," she said still trying to process what he'd said. "I should have listened to you. I won't look into it anymore."

"It's too late now, someone sees you as a threat."

She shook her head, hating the anger and fear in his voice. "No, I'm safe now."

"We'll have the police trace the text, but I'm not too hopeful they'll get anything. We won't pretend that this was done by an amateur. We'll let the police look into it, but I don't have much hope." He walked to the door.

"Sebastian?"

He stopped and turned to her. "What?"

She took a deep breath, her pulse racing. "I love you too."

He closed the space between them, gathered her in his arms and held her as she always dreamed he would and when she whispered 'darling' this time it wasn't pretend.

"I don't know what I'd do if I lost you," he said in a low voice.

"I'm sorry I made you angry."

"All that matters is that you're safe."

She drew away. "You said I can be discharged?"

"Yes, but are you sure you're up to it?"

Naomi nodded, pushing away her sheets. "I want to leave here." She lightly touched his cheek. "And spend the night with you."

Chapter Twenty-four

They were both eager to reach Naomi's bedroom the moment they got home, but Josephine met them in the foyer. Her lips tightened at the sight of them holding hands. Her gaze shifted to Naomi. "Are you okay?"

"Yes, thank you I—"

She looked at her son. "Sebastian, there's something I need to tell you."

He gritted his teeth. "Not now."

"It's important," she said then walked into the sitting room.

"Maybe we should do this later," Naomi whispered, releasing his hand.

He let out a heavy sigh then said, "I'll join you in a minute."

She blew him a kiss. "I'll be waiting."

Sebastian watched her disappear up the stairs, then walked into the other room. "Whatever you have to say had better be very important."

"What's going on between you two?"

He rubbed his hands together annoyed. "Is that what you wanted to discuss? Because if so, I'm leaving."

"I want to know what's going on," Josephine said in a rush when he turned to leave. "Andre told me you found her in the pool."

The concern on her face softened his irritation. He sat down in front of her. "Naomi was attacked because of me."

"Because of you?"

"She was looking into my research at BioCorps."

Josephine rubbed her hand along the arm of her chair. "Why would she do that?"

"Because, for some reason, she thinks I'm innocent."

"I knew she was trouble," Josephine said with a frown. "This must bring back terrible memories for you. How could she be so careless?"

"Her heart was in the right place, but I'll need to keep her close until I find out what's going on."

"I think you should send her away. I don't want her in this house."

"This is my house," he said in a soft voice.

Josephine's voice rose. "Are you choosing her over me?"

"If you don't want to be here you can leave."

Tears sprung to his mother's eyes. "You're throwing me out?"

"Mom, you know you can stay as long as you need, but you can't run my life. If you don't like to see Naomi you can go back to your place."

"Someone attacked her." She pointed to the ground. "Here on our property. What if something happens to you? How do you think I'll bear it?"

"I can take care of myself. You don't have to worry about me. My only concern is Naomi."

"She's gotten a warning, I'm sure if she stops digging nothing else will happen."

"But I can't let it go."

"Why not? You think she knows something?"

"No."

"Then forget it." She leaned forward, clasping her hands together. "Please listen to me. You don't need this. You don't need her. You'd finally gotten your life in order, but you haven't been the same since she came into our lives."

He leaned back in his chair and studied his mother for a long moment before he said, "No, I'm not. I'm not the same man I once was and I have no regrets. She thinks I'm innocent. She believes in me. Her family welcomed me. She talked to me like an equal, something that hasn't happened in a long time."

Josephine sat down beside him and touched his sleeve with tentative fingers. "I know you miss your career, but this isn't the way to get it back. We made an agreement. Can't you forget this and—"

"Is that the man you raised? Do you think I can just walk away after finding out someone lured somebody precious to me and tried to kill her?"

"Sebastian, I'm sure someone was just trying to frighten her."

His eyes blazed, but his voice remained soft. "They may have frightened her, but they made me angry." He stood and stared down at her his voice filled with venom. "And they're going to pay."

Chapter Twenty-five

S ebastian knocked on Naomi's door hoping she was still in the mood. The conversation with his mother had taken longer than he'd planned.

The door swung open. He'd hoped to find her wearing something special—a see-through nightgown, a robe and nothing else—but she wore a long sleeved shirt and jeans. Before he could ask if she'd changed her mind she said, "Are you here for a blow job or a hand job?"

He stood still for a moment then remembered when he'd first shown up at her front door. She'd been wearing the same outfit when she'd thought he'd come for sex. Sebastian let his gaze trail the length of her body. Never had jeans and a plain white shirt looked so sexy before.

He swept her into his arms, closing the door behind him with his foot. "I want it all." He headed for the bedroom.

"I don't do lube jobs."

He laid her down on the bed, took off her glasses, and covered her body with his. "Then we'll have to come up with something else," he said also setting his glasses aside.

Naomi slowly unbuttoned her shirt, trying to display a sophistication she didn't feel. She wanted him so bad, the strength of her feelings frightened her. "Do you have anything particular in mind?"

"I like surprises."

"What did your mother want?"

"I didn't come here to talk about her," he said in a low growl.

Wrong topic, she should have known that, but she had been curious. Her mind had been racing as she waited for him to arrive, wondering if he would or if his mother would convince him to change his mind. But he was here with her, she could claim victory. She'd deal with his mother later.

Naomi removed her shirt then wiggled out of her jeans. "Your mother thinks I'm after your money. I wonder if I should tell her the truth."

"Which is?"

She slid a sensuous path down his chest. "I'm after your body."

"Not my mind?"

"That interests me too, but not at the moment."

Sebastian pressed a finger over her lips. "Don't mention her again. I'm not in the mood to talk about her."

"I bet you don't want to talk at all."

"You're starting to read my mind." He covered her mouth with his and she could feel his erection pressing against her thigh.

It wasn't just his mind she was starting to read. She unbuttoned his trousers and pushed them down. She sighed with relief at the sight of his black boxers. "Thank God," she whispered.

"For what?" he asked, burying his face against her throat, his hand searing a slow, sensuous path down her body.

She closed her eyes, letting the heat build within her. "Promise me you'll never wear striped boxers."

"What if I like stripes?" he asked his breath warm against her skin.

"I don't care."

"Okay, I promise," he said before he kissed her again and his hand slipped inside her panties and with his fingers he made her forget about boxers striped or otherwise.

She rose to meet him and he entered her. She wrapped her legs around him, inviting him deeper inside then the image of Maya with the man's brown bottom in the air flashed in her mind. She swore, unlatched her legs and started to move to the side.

"Whoa, whoa, whoa," Sebastian said. "What are you doing?"

"I want to be on top."

"That's fine, but you've got to let me know." He grinned then winked at her. "We're sorta in this together."

"Right."

They shifted positions. "Better?" he asked.

"Much," she breathed, settling down on him. "I'll make it up to you later."

"You can make it up to me now."

Which she did with gusto. With her mouth she made up for not fulfilling her promise to him right away. With her hands she made up for digging into his past. With her body she made up for all the time she'd held herself back from expressing how she felt. And her feelings came like a tidal wave. No part of him was safe—she was hungry for it all.

And Sebastian didn't drown under her passionate assault. Instead he was a boy in the ocean again—wild and free. Free from ridicule, free from obligation. No longer the boy who'd once been in the wheelchair, or the man who'd disappointed his father, or the scientist who'd lost his career. Naomi swept all those memories away and his heart didn't regret being lost to her.

Together their bodies joined in ecstasy.

"Tell me about the scars," Naomi asked, referring to the scars on his legs, as they lay in each other's arms.

"Lots of surgeries. I was born with extreme clubbed feet."

"Yes, I'd wondered about your walk, you have a unique stride, but I hardly noticed it was a limp," she said quickly when his expression changed. "You've come a long way."

He looked a little rueful. "Just not one hundred percent. I'd fooled myself to think I had."

"I don't need a hundred percent, you're perfect just the way you are." She wrapped her arms tighter around him and sighed with pleasure. "This is nice."

"Only nice?" Sebastian said with an edge of disappointment.

"More than nice. I never thought I could be this happy with someone else."

"I didn't want to quit because of your father."

"What?"

"That night you found me on the kitchen floor, when I said I couldn't take it, it was because of this." He drew her body closer to him. "I wanted this."

"Me too. I thought of kissing your back."

"I thought of kissing more than that," Sebastian said with a dirty laugh.

Naomi sighed. "It's a shame really."

"Why?"

"Because now I really can't work with you anymore."

He looked down at her alarmed. "Why?"

"Conflict of interest and all that."

"I'm a volunteer."

"It's still wrong. I can't have you as my lover and my assistant."

"How about as your husband?"

Naomi stared up at him startled. "You're serious?"

He nodded.

She bit her lip.

"It doesn't have to be now," Sebastian said, sensing her hesitation.

"I can't marry you until—"

"I don't expect you to change your name. I know my reputation will be an issue."

She sat up and looked down at him amazed. "You really are clueless."

"About what?"

She affectionately patted his face. "You're like a frog who still thinks he's a tadpole."

"A frog?"

She nodded.

He frowned. "What does that have to do with whether you'll marry me or not? There's something about me—"

"That's my point. If I marry you, I'd have a stellar lab, a beautiful home, a wonderful man, and work I adore… and you think I'm hesitating because of what happened at BioCorps?"

"I'm Dr. Disgrace, remember? You want to know the truth. You want to know the kind of man I really am."

"I told you, I only did it to help you. I will stop looking, I promise."

His frown increased. "If it's not that, then what is it?"

She let her gaze fall. "I have to deal with something else first."

"What?"

"I can't tell you yet."

"Why not?"

"If…if I can't handle it on my own, I'll let you know."

"I don't like you keeping things from me."

"I know, but what if I say 'yes' and then you change your mind?"

"I won't change my mind."

Naomi sighed. "Give me a week and then we'll see."

His face spread into a wide grin. "So you will marry me?"

"Sebastian, I just said—"

"You're worried I'll change my mind." He shook his head. "I won't," he said before he kissed her, giving her no chance to argue.

Chapter Twenty-six

Vera pinned Naomi with a dark look. "Married?"

They sat in the same café that they had been in weeks before, this time Vera wore a light coat to shield her against the autumn weather settling in, chilling the air and touching the leaves with color.

"Yes."

"When?"

"We haven't discussed it."

"Who?"

"He's also a scientist."

"Didn't I warn you about that? Did the breakup of my marriage teach you nothing? A woman in your position must choose a man from a different field. There's bound to be jealousy when one's career grows faster than another's. What does he do exactly?"

"Right now he's not in the field. But I do see him returning to it."

"Who is he?"

"Sebastian Scott."

"No."

"What?"

"Not only is he not a scientist, he's the lowest sort of man you can attach yourself to."

"I don't think so, although I wasn't able to prove that there might have been a mistake at BioCorps I believe—"

"Are you even listening to yourself? You're already putting your career behind a man who couldn't even handle his own. You made a narrow mistake with Barry. Two kids in three years."

"She's happy."

"Does she have a choice?"

"Of course she does. She wanted a family."

"A man will saddle you down, even the best of them. If it's not children, it's the weight of their career or the delicacy of their ego."

"Not all men."

"A man like Sebastian Scott will drag you down. Don't think I haven't noticed the pretty glass cage he's slowly been putting you in. The house, the lab."

Naomi shook her head. "I didn't—"

"Gifts like that always come with a price. You can only trust your own hard work and effort."

"I do work hard."

"Then why is Pete O'Connell able to get the brightest researchers?"

"Because, through Sebastian, I've learned that our field isn't only about being the brightest and having the most stellar reputation. It's also about being liked and respected. I've had to learn to treat my team better. Give them compliments once in a while." She hadn't done this before

Sebastian, she'd taken her researchers for granted and the people who funded her work. She'd been blind to the needs of others, not realizing what a kind gesture or word could do.

"Do you hand out lollipops too?"

Naomi sighed. "I didn't come here to ask for your blessing, I wanted advice."

"And I'm giving it to you. Don't go after a man like a starry eyed teenager. You're a scientist letting your heart rule your head."

"I wanted to know more about Josephine Scott."

"Who?"

"His mother."

"Are you still looking into BioCorps?"

"No, I just wanted to know if—"

"Why would I know anything about her? I've told you this and I'll say it again. Sebastian Scott is poison and that includes those around him. Stay away."

"Why? One man's meat—"

"Is another man's poison," Vera finished in a grave tone. "I don't believe in taking gambles." She stood. "And neither should you."

Naomi finished her coffee disappointed as she watched her friend leave the shop. She'd hoped to be able to get help from Vera, but she would have to face the problem she faced alone.

Naomi found Josephine in her favorite position in the solarium reading.

"I want to marry your son, but I need to understand something first."

"What is that?"

"Why did you try to kill me?"

Chapter Twenty-seven

"I don't know what you mean."

"I felt the edge of your cane that night. And I heard the sound of your footsteps. I know it wasn't Andre's and Sebastian's walk is very distinctive. I know it was you."

Josephine sniffed. "You can't prove a thing."

"So you did do it."

Her lips thinned.

"You hate me that much?" When Josephine remained mute, Naomi sighed and said, "If you won't give me any answers, I'll tell Sebastian my suspicions."

"You can't tell him," she demanded. "I wouldn't have let you die. I had no other choice. It was him or you."

"What do you mean?"

"Why must you ask so many questions? Why couldn't you have left things alone?"

"I don't know who you're trying to protect."

"Him. I've always done everything for him. He was happy as things were before you came into our lives."

"No, he wasn't. He wouldn't have sought me out otherwise."

"He had a moment of weakness, nothing more."

"You're not answering my question. Do you hate me that much?"

"Yes, because you're a threat. I need Sebastian here as the head of his father's business. BioCorps nearly destroyed him, I won't see that happen again."

"Mrs. Scott—"

"I'll make you a bargain. I won't interfere with you two as long as you never tell him what happened."

"And why would I do that?"

"Because if you want him to stay with you, you'll keep this a secret."

A secret. *I don't like you not telling me things,* he'd said. But would he believe her if she did?

She could imagine his reaction. He'd deny it at first. Tell her she was mistaken. Force her to provide proof. All she had was her memory. That wouldn't be enough and he'd get angry at her for accusing his mother of something awful. She remembered the rage in his eyes at the hospital when he thought of the person who'd put her there. Would he turn that rage on her? He'd never look at her the same way again.

But if she didn't tell him, he'd never know the depth of his mother's manipulation. How much she hated his love of science. At times, Naomi wondered if Josephine had something to do with the fall of Sebastian's career. But it was all speculation and she had no proof. Vera had warned her that Sebastian was poison and all those around him. Did she know what Josephine was capable of?

But a secret would slowly erode their relationship. Is that what his mother really wanted?

She shook her head. "No, I—"

"Stop pretending," Josephine snapped.

"What?"

"Stop pretending you don't know what happened. Did they put you up to this? Wasn't ruining his career enough for them?"

"Enough for whom? I don't know what you're talking about?"

"You really want me to believe that all this time they haven't mentioned anything? Were they using you to make sure that he didn't say anything?"

"Who are they? I don't understand."

"You keep acting as if you know what he needs when all this time you've been close to the very person who ended Sebastian's career."

"I haven't been close to anyone who could hurt him."

Josephine's lip curled. "Except Vera Conklin."

Chapter Twenty-eight

Bad news. He always knew when someone was going to give him bad news and Andre didn't disappoint.

"The jeweler mixed up the order. It won't be ready."

Sebastian hit the steering wheel of his car as he made his way back home after dropping Naomi off at work. She'd been quiet that morning and he'd hoped his gift—a ruby necklace—would have cheered her up when he gave it to her that evening.

"What do you want me to do?"

"They'd better give me a discount, bonus or something impressive if they want to keep my business."

"I'll let them know."

He heard Andre hesitate and knew there was further bad news. "What else?"

"I have to run some errands for your mother, but the security company that you wanted to install cameras around the pool said they'd be coming in an hour."

"I'm almost home, I'll handle it."

Moments later, he stormed into the house.

"What are you doing home so early?" his mother asked surprised. "You look upset."

"Because Naomi's—"

"Whatever she told you about me is a lie."

He paused. "Excuse me?"

"Naomi." Josephine nervously licked her lips. "What did she say?"

Naomi hadn't said anything, but from the guilty look on his mother's face, she should have. He folded his arms. "Let me hear it from you."

"I knew she couldn't keep her mouth shut. You know I only did it for you."

He nodded. "Yes, you always try to protect me."

"And she was being dramatic. I was trying to scare her, not kill her."

Sebastian felt his body grow cold. "The pool?"

"Yes, I pushed her, but that hardly qualifies for homicidal intent."

"You're the one who attacked her?"

"Yes," Josephine said suddenly hesitant. "Isn't that what she told you?"

"No," Sebastian said, drawing out the word and narrowing his eyes. "She didn't, but I knew something was wrong." He rested his hands on his hips. "I can't believe what I just heard. You tried to kill her?"

"I didn't try to kill anybody! They said I had to do something."

"Who?"

"You know who. I had to do something so when Andre told me you'd had a fight with Naomi, I took a gamble. I didn't really think it would work to be honest. I spoofed your phone and sent a text to her. I kept waiting for something to go wrong, but it didn't. So when she showed up, I took my chance."

"You left her floating in the pool."

"I wouldn't have let her die, I swear. I was scared of what they would do to you."

"If Vera and Niklaas threatened you, why didn't you come to me?"

"Because you're under her spell, I didn't think you'd listen to me."

Sebastian nodded as the pieces fell into place. "You're the reason she's afraid to marry me." He turned. "I have to talk to her."

Josephine grabbed his hand. "You know I did it for you. Your father dreamed of you running the business—"

"I don't want to run the business! Don't you understand? I never have. I only did it because at the time I felt it was the right choice, but not anymore."

"How can you turn away from all that your father built for you and your brother? How can you cast aside all that he sacrificed?"

"Dad loved what he did. It wasn't a sacrifice for him, it was a pleasure. I don't feel the same, never have." He took a deep steadying breath. "We'll discuss this later. I have to talk to Naomi right now." He turned to the door.

"I told her about Vera Conklin."

Sebastian spun around, stunned that his mother would put Naomi in such a dangerous position. "How much did you tell her?"

Josephine flashed a cruel grin. "Enough to make her curious."

Chapter Twenty-nine

Naomi had expected a gun or a knife, but the syringe in Vera's hand seemed oddly perfect. She'd left her lab to visit Vera in her office and confront her about what Josephine had shared. Vera had welcomed her into the sleek, minimalist room with the same cool detachment Naomi had grown used to.

She sat at the round table in the corner where two coffee cups sat, prepared to get answers. How could Vera be the reason for Sebastian's dismissal? What had really happened?

But when Vera sat down in front of her and pulled out the syringe, Naomi knew she shouldn't have come. The woman she'd trusted wasn't all that she'd seemed.

"I warned you," she said, when she saw Naomi look at the object in her hand. "You were always so tenacious. Always looking deeper and closer than you should. Why couldn't you have left things as they were?"

"Sebastian knows I'm here," she lied.

"No, he doesn't. He wouldn't have let you come. You came here all on your own without telling anyone. I know you Naomi. You're one who's proud to depend on herself."

"Sebastian will—"

"I'll deal with Sebastian just as I did all those years ago."

"You don't need to do this. I still don't know what happened."

Vera shrugged. "Your suspicions are enough to make you dangerous."

Suspicions. What did Vera suspect that she knew? How could she be involved? Did it have anything to do with her former husband? She had to keep her talking as she tried to figure a way to get out. "Why did you do it?" she asked, still not knowing what 'it' was.

"I fell under the very spell I warned you about."

"You fell for a man who promised you the world," Naomi guessed. "A man you'd do anything for."

"A man?" Vera said with a note of derision. "It was Niklaas who nearly ruined everything. I had to protect his reputation and mine. What would have happened to me if Niklaas' mistake was uncovered? All the years would have been washed away. Scott had his father's money to fall back on, we had nothing."

"So you made a deal," Naomi guessed.

"That was his mother's idea. Scott had shared his concerns regarding Niklaa's performance with her. He was the one who discovered Niklaas had made a major miscalculation with the data, which would cost BioCorps millions to fix. He told his mother and she helped devise a plan. Josephine used her connections within the media to persuade the public relations division of BioCorps to carefully state what had happened. Scott fell on his sword, so to speak, because he respected Niklaas so much and his father was dying so his mother persuaded him to give up his science career and fulfill his father's wish to head the company he'd built for him and his brother.

"But in the end it had been a waste. Niklaas already had years behind him and had lost his enthusiasm. Scott was the more brilliant scientist. He would have done more in five years than Niklaas could in twenty." She shrugged. "But talking about the past bores me. So—"

Naomi lifted up the table, startling Vera and giving her enough time to try to escape. She ran to the door and struggled to unlock it, but Vera grabbed her before she could. Vera grabbed her arm, dragging her back. Naomi pulled out of her jacket and dove for the door again, her bare arm now exposed.

Vera grabbed her leg, causing Naomi to drop to the ground.

"There's no use trying to fight me," she said, saddling Naomi, effectively pinning her to the ground. She held down Naomi's arm and lifted the syringe.

Naomi slid her other arm free and yanked Vera's earring from her ear, tearing through the flesh. Vera screamed out in shock and pain, giving Naomi enough time to shift Vera's body and knock her to the ground, the syringe scattered to the ground.

They both lunged for it, Vera getting it first. She held it like a knife while Naomi gripped her wrist, her hand trembling as the syringe drew slowly, closer to her skin. Vera was bigger, stronger. Naomi knew she couldn't win by sheer might, she had to use surprise. So she went limp, dropping to the ground, still holding Vera's hand and causing her to stab herself in the thigh.

Vera stared at the needle horrified. "You bitch," she cried, yanking it out.

Naomi surged to her feet and ran, this time managing to open the door before Vera could reach her. She rushed into the hallway and saw Sebastian coming from the other end. "Naomi!"

She ran into his arms.

Chapter Thirty

The ruby necklace settled beautifully around Naomi's neck, while the soft sounds of the Caribbean Sea drifted on a wave of a floral scented wind that drifted through their hotel window.

"Do you like it?" Sebastian asked, meeting Naomi's eye in the mirror reflection.

She lightly touched the exquisite piece. "It's beautiful."

After the horror of what had happened in Vera's office she was afraid she'd never feel awe, joy or safe again. Sebastian couldn't seem to hold her close enough to rid her of the feeling. She still shivered with fear at the thought that Vera had tried to kill her; that Josephine had pushed her in the water. In her nightmares, sometimes she was drowning; other times she was being stabbed, every time Sebastian woke her and soothed her back to sleep.

When she learned that Vera survived—barely—she felt a sense of relief. She hadn't wanted to have killed her; the courts would judge her instead and she'd suffer some long lingering effects of the poison. Josephine apologized to Naomi, with Sebastian's urging, and reluctantly accepted her son's decision to hire someone else to run the company, while he devoted his attention to helping Dr. Mensah with the research for his book.

Naomi remembered the sound of autumn leaves scattering along the ground while she and Sebastian stood in front of his father's grave—a large monument to a life well lived. Sebastian held her hand and solemnly introduced her before he said, "We didn't agree on a lot of things, Dad, but I think you'd agree that I made a good choice. You'd like her." He took a deep breath, blinking back tears. "It was a long time coming, but I'm happy now and I wish you could be here and see me as a man you could be proud of."

Naomi squeezed his hand and said in a soft voice. "I think you were already that man five years ago. You're just finally realizing that now."

A ghost of a smile touched his lips and he nodded. "Your right," he said and the weight she'd sensed he'd been carrying melted away.

But even as she stood in a white organza wedding dress staring up at him as they said their vows, a fear still gripped her—a fear she couldn't shake. She didn't feel safe. She felt she could still lose him somehow.

Now, as she felt the weight of his hands on her shoulders as they stood together in front of the mirror in their honeymoon suite, she finally identified her true fear. "I don't know if I'll ever love you enough." She turned to him, meeting his steady brown gaze. "I haven't changed. I can still be absentminded. I might miss birthdays or anniversaries, dinner dates and be late for vacations."

He smiled amused. "I'll keep you on schedule."

"But if I forget, I don't want you to be angry with me. My family is used to me, but…I don't want you to think that I don't—"

He cupped her chin, his voice tender. "I won't get angry about any of that. I love you too much to care."

Naomi felt her anxiety slip away under his warm, gentle gaze. A buoyant joy filled her heart; she could still make mistakes and have him by her side. "Is that a promise?"

"Yes, I promise," he said then sealed it with a kiss.

About the Author

Dara Girard is an award-winning, national bestselling author of more than thirty books including *Unexpected Pleasure, Just One Look, The Amber Stone* and *Dangerous Curves.* Dara loves to travel and hear from readers.

You can write her at:
contactdara@daragirard.com
or
P.O. Box 10345
Silver Spring, MD 20914

If you'd like to receive a reply, please send a self-addressed stamped envelope. Visit daragirard.com to join her newsletter and be the first to find out about current and upcoming releases.